Ian Stuart

Politics in Performance

The Production Work of Edward Bond, 1978–1990

PETER LANG
New York • Washington, D.C./Baltimore
Bern • Frankfurt am Main • Berlin • Vienna • Paris

Library of Congress Cataloging-in-Publication Data

Stuart, Ian.
Politics in performance: the production work
of Edward Bond, 1978–1990/
Ian Stuart.
p. cm. — (Artists and issues in the theatre; v. 6)
Includes bibliographical references and index.
1. Bond, Edward—Political and social views. 2. Politics and literature—Great
Britain—History—20th century. 3. Political plays, English—History and
criticism. 4. Theater—Political aspects—Great Britain. 5. Bond, Edward—
Dramatic production. 6. Theater—Production and direction. 7. Bond,
Edward—Stage history. I. Title. II. Series: Artists and
issues in the theatre; vol. 6.
PR6052. 05Z924   822'.914—dc20   95-33108
ISBN 0-8204-3014-5
ISSN 1051-9718

Die Deutsche Bibliothek-CIP-Einheitsaufnahme

Stuart, Ian:
Politics in performance: the production work of Edward Bond, 1978–1990/
Ian Stuart. – New York; Washington, D.C./Baltimore; Bern;
Frankfurt am Main; Berlin; Vienna; Paris: Lang.
(Artists and issues in the theatre; Vol. 6)
ISBN 0-8204-3014-5
NE: GT

The paper in this book meets the guidelines for permanence and durability
of the Committee on Production Guidelines for Book Longevity
of the Council of Library Resources.

Printed in the United States of America.

Acknowledgment

My thanks to Professors Robert G. Egan, Robert Potter, and Judith Olauson, in the Department of Dramatic Art, University of California, Santa Barbara, who guided this work through its initial stages; the actors and directors met in connection with this study; Tim Kedge without whose support and encouragement *Politics in Performance: The Production Work of Edward Bond 1978-1990* would never have been completed. I owe a special debt of gratitude to Edward and Elisabeth Bond-Pablé and to my parents who followed my progress with love and encouragement.

This book is dedicated to the memory of a former director, actor, and teacher, Geoff Pywell Ph.D., his wife and son, who were tragically killed in an automobile accident, Labor Day 1995.

Table of Contents

Introduction

Edward Bond is among Britain's most controversial left-wing dramatists. However, unlike his contemporaries, Howard Brenton, David Edgar and Trevor Griffiths to name just a few, since 1978 Bond has been committed to directing the first productions of his new plays. Crossing the divide from writer to director is a complex matter. Bond has admitted that this transition may be seen as implying a lack of trust in actors and directors who work on his plays.[1] But this is not the case. Bond's real motive is a genuine desire to understand the difficulties of actors. As a writer he appreciates that his texts may pose fundamental problems to the creative artist. Therefore, by directing his own work, Bond believes it is possible to discover the origin of these difficulties and solve them in his writing. In an article which appeared in 1985, Bond clearly stated his reasons for directing:

> There is a great temptation just to say to oneself stay at home, write your plays, and then if they are of use somebody may be sufficiently interested in producing them. But that would be bad for me as a writer. I would just stop. I need that physical experience because it feeds back into my subsequent plays.[2]

The phenomenon of a writer directing his own work is not unusual. What is unusual is a writer who states that he *needs* to direct for the benefit of his writing and who is actively engaged in formulating his own acting theories. Bond has observed the significance of directing the initial productions of his plays:

> The reason why I want to direct my plays is that they are experimental without being obviously so. . . In order to write better for actors, I have to become part of their rehearsal process. If I want actors to be of a different sort, I have to get involved in the actual technique of creating it with the actor. I can't any longer be in the situation of nudging someone and getting them to relay the message. It's simpler and more economic if I do it myself. Once the play has been done, and I've been

able to understand what all the operational problems are, I can then revise and put instructions in the text.[3]

Bond's plays in performance require an alternative approach to acting that necessitates his close directorial involvement:

> The plays are making new demands on actors—and I need circumstances in which I can work this out. . . The purpose of being on stage has to change and so does the nature, the object, of acting. And so does the text—which functions in new ways.[4]

Some actors have stated that Bond's involvement in the rehearsal process stems from an inability to release his work to actors and directors.[5] In a letter Bond clarifies his position:

> When I direct or attend rehearsals of one of my plays I make one thing clear: I do not know how to play it. That is not my job. The joy of theatre is that the real secrets of a role lie in the performer not in the text—and I'm too selfish to give up that joy. All I can do is make clear the situations and their implications. If these are falsified there is a moral morass and, interestingly, no drama. Surely an encouraging connection between drama and truth! Yet our theatre is being destroyed by just such falsifications, and by directors who try stunt lighting, and coercive music and other effects that please and even stun but in the end stupefy. Effect-and-effect is replacing cause-and-effect.[6]

The purpose of this study is to explore the productions on which Bond has worked or advised and assess to what extent his theories of acting have been realized in practice. In addition, the physical and visual elements of Bond's productions, from *The Woman* in 1978 until *Jackets* in 1989/90, will be examined.

The twentieth century has seen the emergence of two leading theoreticians of acting—Konstantin Stanislavsky and Bertolt Brecht. Bond has described Stanislavsky's work as "important" but "misunderstood":

> In America his [Stanislavsky's] method has degenerated into the "treatment"—a way of injecting false lies into morbid and sterile artistic philosophies.[7]

Bond also remarks on the significance of Brecht's acting theories but observes that they are "not an adequate description of the way what happens on the stage relates to an audience."[8] Before examining Bond's acting theories, it is important to explore the acting techniques advocated by Stanislavsky and Brecht and assess the influences on Bond's approach to acting.

Konstantin Stanislavsky created a "system" of acting in the early part of the twentieth century which still occupies an important place in contemporary theatre.[9] Although his working methodology underwent revisions during his lifetime, Stanislavsky maintained a belief in the importance of an actor creating theatrical truth in his work. This meant replacing the Delsartean-based gestures of feeling with behavior that was, within the constraints of the theatre, a believable reflection of life.[10] To accomplish this, Stanislavsky introduced a process which developed the inner and outer work of the actor. The actor's inner work mainly consists of psychological exercises intended to arouse an inner state of creativity. The outer work of the actor concentrated on the physical and vocal embodiment of the character. These inner exercises included a study of objectives, physical actions, given circumstances and the creative "if" developed to assist the actor in releasing his unconscious energies and revealing the psychological truth of the character. Stanislavsky's "system" also discusses an actor's work on his role. This was a more external exploration of an actor's work suggesting a particular method of constructing a role through extensive study of the character and play.

If Stanislavsky sought to unite the actor and his character, Brecht's aim was to distance the actor from his role. "A Dialogue about Acting" published by the *Berliner Borsen-Courier* in February 1929, contained Brecht's attack on an approach to acting that he thought was designed to manipulate the audience's emotional response:

> (Actors perform at the moment) by means of hypnosis. They go into a trance and take the audience with them. Suppose they have to act a leave-taking. They put themselves in a leave-taking mood. They want to induce a leave-taking mood in the audience. If the seance is successful it ends up with nobody seeing anything further, nobody learning any lessons, at best everyone recollecting. In short, everyone feels.[11]

Stanislavsky and his approach are mentioned by Brecht in an article appearing in 1957. Here Brecht suggests that an actor cannot "feel" the emotions of the character he is playing:

He soon gets exhausted and begins just to copy various superficialities
of the other person's speech and hearing, whereupon the effect on the
public drops off alarmingly. . . The subconscious is not at all responsive
to guidance; it has as it were a bad memory.[12]

Brecht's approach to acting is summed up in his "Short
Description of a New Technique of Acting which Produces an
Alienation Effect," which appeared in 1951. On stage, the actor
emphasizes that he is not transformed into his character but
instead "demonstrates" him as authentically as possible. This is
a point Brecht makes in his famous statement about the "Street
Scene":

In short, the actor must remain a demonstrator; he must present the
person demonstrated as a stranger, he must not suppress the "*he* did
that, not go so far as to be wholly transformed into the person demonstrated.[13]

As the actor does not have to assume the character's personal-
ity, Brecht maintains that he should have a definite position
about the character. In Brecht's form of theatre, a significant
characteristic is that nothing is hidden. In the article, Brecht
emphasized the significance of gesture:

The actor has to find a sensibly perceptible outward expression for his
character's emotions, preferably some action that gives away what is
going on inside him. The emotion in question must be brought out,
must lose all its restrictions so that it can be treated on a big scale.[14]

No concealment or hidden method should be adopted by the
actor; an audience should be able to see the actor's skill, like
that of an acrobat. Titles should be used on a screen and both
the actor and production share a "historical quality." By this
Brecht means the attitude historians adopt to the facts of a
bygone era. In his opinion, actors should have a similar view
based on treating old ideas with a fresh perspective. For Brecht,
the significance of his approach to acting lies in its ability to
"make strange" elements from an audience's world which at
first sight may appear familiar:

Characters and incidents from ordinary life, from our immediate surroundings, being familiar, strike us more or less as natural. Alienating
them helps us to make them seem remarkable to us.[15]

Brecht wanted a theatre which made the "ordinary, familiar and immediately accessible into something peculiar, striking and unexpected."[16] In doing this, Brecht believed his theatre went at least one stage further than Stanislavsky's by presenting more than just theatrical truth. In Brecht's opinion, it was within the theatre's potential to change an audience's reaction to its customary surroundings. Therefore, he attempted to remove the "mystical elements that have stuck to the orthodox theatre from the old days" and show that people were capable of changing their reality.[17]

A Brechtian acting-style is often misinterpreted as emotionless. This is not the case, as Brecht has suggested: "It would be quite wrong to try and deny emotion to this kind of theatre."[18] The difference between Brecht and Stanislavsky is that the emotional response given by a Brechtian actor is intended to be political. According to Brecht:

> The emotions always have a definite class basis; the form they take at any time is historical, restricted and limited in specific ways. The emotions are in no sense universally human and timeless.[19]

Edward Bond rejects this notion that the lives of individuals are shaped by their unconscious experiences:

> We are not little paper-boat consciousness swilling around on a huge dark sea of the unconscious. That is not true at all. We have to earn our living and so we might go and make bombs in order to blow up people and ensure that others will make bombs and come and blow us up. That is how you earn your living in an arms factory. Its not got any deep psychological drive towards evil.[20]

Bond states that Brecht "believed that a character should be shown not so much as an individual but as a class function," whereas his form of theatre connects psychological truth to an individual's class position.[21] This method of showing the truth about the nature of political relationships is the most significant difference between Brecht's and Bond's acting theories. Bond's philosophy is worth quoting in full as it helps to separate his approach to theatre from that of Brecht:

> At the moment, in our society as it is, the truth is more terrible than a caricature of it. To show this truth, just as to show the mask under the

face, we need a new way of acting, one that will not simplify the complexities of experience by abstracting from it but will let us make the total complexity of a character simple and understandable. After all, that is what self-consciousness does when it develops into political consciousness, into class consciousness, in working people. Self-consciousness then becomes self-manipulative because it has then become a body of concepts, ideas, precepts, tests and experience which have been shown to be valid in critical, defining situations. If this insight and understanding could be used to develop a form of acting that could demonstrate truth to the audience, that would be the most important advance our theatre could make.[22]

It must be made clear that Bond's attempt to link psychological truth with a character's class consciousness does not negate emotion. Like Stanislavsky's theories of acting and Brecht's drama in practice, I have seen that Bond's work demands an emotional charge from both the actor and its audience. For example in the National Theatre's 1982 production of *Summer*, Yvonne Bryceland, playing Marthe, did not simply act the part of a dying woman. Instead, through the actress' skill and versatility, the audience's attention was drawn to the contradiction of Marthe's life: she was alive in Xenia's dead world. However, Bond's concern lies in the purpose of producing an emotional response. Bond expresses his point of view in a way that might have been shared by Stanislavsky and Brecht:

When it comes to acting on stage, I feel very strongly that the actor needs to be emotional, that he should have an emotional response to what he is doing just as he should have an emotional love for what he is doing. But I feel that he shouldn't be driven by the emotion that's all. . . You must use an emotion to show us something more than you are just having an emotion.[23]

In this way, Bond believes that feelings will not just be shown as free-floating but something firmly rooted in class experience. Wanda Rulewicz states in *A Semiotic Study of Edward Bond*:

Bond wants his actors to act lives, not abstractions, since, in his opinion, one of the main strengths of drama might otherwise be wasted. Class functions must be shown and it is necessary to extend the ways of showing them.[24]

Throughout the practical work on his plays, Bond has developed an acting style. This approach was consciously manifested in the PS—Public Soliloquy—concept in *The Worlds*, TEs—Theatre Events—and "T" acting during rehearsals for *The War Plays* and *Jackets*, although Bond maintains this style has always been present in his work:

> I think I have always dealt in TEs but it is something that I have begun to elaborate on and be more conscious about, more conscious in order to become more intensive of course.[25]

TEs and "T" acting will be explored in relationship to the six British productions on which Bond has worked. In the meantime, the central characteristics of these terms should be defined.

In his study of Bond, David L. Hirst offers a definition of the Public Soliloquy:

> [The Public Soliloquy provides] moments of hightened [sic] insight when a character, responding to his circumstances, sees beyond the immediate situation he deepens his self-awareness by intensifying his consciousness of his own position and that of others in society.[26]

These elevated moments are what Bond terms the PS. He suggests that the PS contains fully digested thoughts which can be used as a guide to interpretation of the character. Bond has described an approach to the PS which demonstrates their significance in performance:

> Think of the speeches not as final accomplishments; but as recipes applied retrospectively—they speak (like a cook) the recipe and retrospectively their lives are lived/created (are/have been) by the recipes. Or you could say they were living in order to make that moment.[27]

TEs can be described as exploiting "a scene or sequence in order to illustrate the meaning of what is happening":

> The TE should use theatre to illustrate, illuminate, make physical and imagistic what is ordinarily mundane: the silent scream is more than just another scream. The TE activates theatre—makes theatre theatrical as it were. The audience then have a sense of being at the theatre. . . In the TE the audience become practitioners.[28]

In essence, TEs can be described as strong visual moments for an audience which are primarily intellectual but also emotion-

ally significant. Bond maintains TEs have always been present
in his work:

> My plays are absolutely saturated with TEs, like the tin cans in the final
> scene of *The Pope's Wedding*. This is my first play and they are there. It
> seems to me that is something that has been presented to me by an
> awareness of a society that I have been born in, am writing in and will
> die in because it will not change before then. I think you will find lots
> of places in my plays where you can find TEs.[29]

According to Bond: "TEs can join the abstract, the material and
the particular in useful ways in that they should always show the
most immediate, hum-drum, mundane details."[30] In an interview, Bond provided further clarification concerning the TE:

> TEs take the unexpected and absolutely show that. If I were showing a
> coronation, I would show the Archbishop of Canterbury cleaning his
> nails the night before and then as he puts the crown on you see his
> nails among the jewels. . . I think that TEs are an attempt to invent a
> new language. You produce the TE and then that is the audience's
> work.[31]

Bond maintains that "TEs are not arbitrary. The text suggests
them."[32]

This notion of the practical function of theatre is also central
to Bond's idea of "T" acting. "T" acting is a concept of social
rationality which can be seen in the acting of Bond's productions as early as *The Woman* in 1978. The concept can be
defined as a desire by an actor not to conceal the play's meaning but reveal its structure which is then developed by an audience—what Bond has termed AW, audience work. Bond has
commented:

> If you don't put on stage what our involvement in life is then I don't
> think the audience has proper work to do in the theatre. They become
> mere spectators rather than participants.[33]

But how does Bond's theory of acting work in practice? Bond
developed these concepts in a series of acting workshops conducted at the National Theatre in 1981.

Held on three Saturday mornings for students, the workshops involved two professional actors, Yvonne Bryceland and
Philip Davis. In addition to putting Bond's acting theory into

practice, the workshops also developed the questions Bond needed to ask of actors:

> An actor presumably will act a solution to certain questions which he puts to himself and what you've got to do is alter the questions he puts to himself. It seems to me that one wants a more graphic form of acting. A form of acting that is more, in a sense, pictorial.[34]

Davis recalls an exercise which he took part in during the workshops:

> I remember working through *The Bundle*, the bit where he discovers the child and throws it back into the river. We did it in various ways. One was just to let me do it as I would have "realistically" done it. Of course, I did it very sentimentally, that there was this man ripped apart by guilt. In doing that I made the action irrational. Then we did it another way, the speech was done acknowledging the audience. It was all done demonstrably, showing the meaning of the speech rather than playing the person in the situation.[35]

Although these acting exercises pre-date Bond's conscious use of TEs, they do have a connection with them. Bond was attempting to discover moments which captured the dynamics of a social situation. By injecting a political dynamic into the scene, Bond was attempting to find an alternative iconography for the exercise.

Bond's first opportunity for directing his own work occurred in Vienna at the Burgtheater in January 1973. He directed *Lear* with settings by Hayden Griffin, who was to design *The Woman*, *The Worlds*, *Restoration* and *Summer*, and Andy Phillips, lighting designer at Britain's National Theatre. The production of *Lear* has not been discussed in any detail in this study because there were no detectable advances during rehearsals toward the evolution of acting style. Bond has commented on the negative aspects of this experience:

> I was directing in an incredibly conservative theatre. It really was a question of learn your words and apply your skills to them. Quite what I achieved is difficult to know. The rehearsal situation was very bad. For example, I can remember one rehearsal where someone had to drop down dead. Before she fell down, an attendant walked on with a blanket for her to fall on. I doubt whether I made any advances in acting theory for this production.[36]

A subsequent production, *After the Assassinations*, has also not been covered in this book. A student production at the University of Essex in 1983, Bond has described the experience as being "a total waste for everyone."[37] Little progress was made in this production toward discovering a style of presentation, and a full text of the play is unavailable. Consequently, this study focuses on the six British productions of his plays on which Bond has spent major creative energy. All of these plays have received professional premieres and eventuated in published texts.

In this study I have attempted to give the reader a total sense of the production. A significant part of the reconstruction process has been provided by Edward Bond, his letters, artistic collaborators and the actors from the productions. The six plays covered are: *The Woman*, which opened at the National Theatre on August 10, 1978; *The Worlds*, which received productions by students in Newcastle on March 8, 1979 and the Activist's Youth Theatre Club at the Royal Court Theatre Upstairs, London on November 21, 1979, as well as a professional production, directed by Nick Hamm, which opened at the New Half Moon Theatre on June 16, 1981; *Restoration*, which opened at the Royal Court Theatre on July 21, 1981 and the Royal Shakespeare Company's revival on September 13, 1988; *Summer*, which opened at the National Theatre on January 27, 1982; *The War Plays*, a trilogy, Parts One and Two opening on May 29, 1985 and the third section on July 17, 1985 by the Royal Shakespeare Company at the Pit in the Barbican; and *Jackets*, both parts of which were directed by Keith Sturgess at the University of Lancaster on January 24, 1989 and the second part receiving its professional premiere, directed by Nick Philippou on October 23, 1989. This production of *Jackets II* was a touring production beginning at the University of East Anglia and concluding twenty-five venues later with a two week run opening at the Haymarket Studio Theatre, Leicester on November 28, 1989. In the cases of the New Half Moon production of *The Worlds*, the RSC's *Restoration* and the London *Jackets*, I have included in this study productions not directed by Bond but which had substantial assistance from him during rehearsals.

My own interest in Edward Bond's plays, poems, writings and productions began in January, 1982 as an undergraduate at Bretton Hall College in England. A colleague wrote to Bond with a series of questions about acting and theatre. Bond replied at length to the letter on tape and all the drama students listened to his answers. I remember thinking that here was a playwright passionately interested in developing an acting style for the production of his plays. I obtained a copy of the recording, and some of that material is used in this study. In his response, Bond challenged and overturned traditional views of acting:

> Most of the processes actors go through in order to create a character seem to me to be verging on the idiotic. They are of no use to me. So I have to try and work out a way of relating to actors and helping them to understand the new sorts of roles I am writing.[38]

I was intrigued by this figure who criticized acting techniques but who, at the time, seemed to have only a vague notion of how to improve upon them.

After seeing Bond's production of *Summer* at the National Theatre in 1982, I became convinced that Bond was attempting to discover an alternative acting style. Since then, I have closely followed Bond's development as a writer and director in his productions of *The War Plays* and *Jackets*. During rehearsals for these two plays, Bond strengthened his concepts of TEs and "T" acting, the approach to acting which he first mentioned in those taped remarks some years earlier.

Notes

1 Edward Bond, taped correspondence to John Lamb, January 1982.

2 Edward Bond quoted in "Edward Bond British Secret Playwright," by Malcolm Hay. *Plays and Players* June 1985: 9.

3 Edward Bond, unpublished interview with Patricia Curran, 1 July 1979, quoted in *Bond on File*, compiled by Philip Roberts, (London: Methuen, 1985) 74.

4 Edward Bond, letter to Max Stafford-Clark, 24 April 1990.

5 For example, Anna Massey, "Across the Water," *Plays and Players*, July 1991: 12.

6 Edward Bond, letter to the Editor, *Plays and Players*, 4 August 1991.

7 Edward Bond, letter to Oleg Yefremov, 13 February 1989.

8 Edward Bond, personal interview, 12 June 1990.

9 See Konstantin Stanislavsky, *An Actor Prepares*, trans., Elizabeth Reynolds Hapgood (New York: Theatre Arts Books, 1952). *Creating a Role* trans., Elizabeth Reynolds Hapgood (New York: Theatre Arts Books, 1949).

10 "Francois Delsarte (1811-1871), reacting against the mechanical and formalized actor training of his time, attempted to return to nature carefully observing and recording those expressions and gestures produced not by art but by instinct and emotion. But when these were codified for his students, the result was yet another mechanical system, the formal details of which were so rigorously taught by Delsarte's disciples for the remainder of the century that even today his system is almost a synonym for mechanical, arbitrary expressions and gestures, the very thing it was created to prevent." Marvin Carlson, *Theories of the Theatre* (Ithaca and London: Cornell University Press, 1984) 218.

11 Bertolt Brecht, "Dialog uber Schauspielkunst," trans., John Willett in *Brecht on Theatre* (London: Methuen, 1974) 26.

12 Bertolt Brecht, "Verfremdungseffekte in der chinesischen Schauspielkunst," trans., John Willett in *Brecht on Theatre* 93/4.

13 Bertolt Brecht, "Die Strassenszene Grundmodell eines epischen Theaters," trans., John Willett in *Brecht on Theatre* 139.

14 Bertolt Brecht, "Kurze Beschreibung einer neuen Technik der Schauspielkunst, die einen Verfremdungseffekt hervorbringt," trans., John Willett in *Brecht on Theatre* 140.

15 Bertolt Brecht, "Kurze Beschreibung einer neuen Technik der Schauspielkunst, die einen Verfremdungseffekt hervorbringt," trans., John Willett in *Brecht on Theatre* 140.

16 Bertolt Brecht, note 17, "Kurze Beschreibung einer neuen Technik der Schauspielkunst, die einen Verfremdungseffekt hervorbringt," trans., John Willett in *Brecht on Theatre* 143.

17 Bertolt Brecht, "Kurze Beschreibung einer neuen Technik der Schauspielkunst, die einen Verfremdungseffekt hervorbringt," trans., John Willett in *Brecht on Theatre* 140.

18 Bertolt Brecht, "Schwierigkeiten des spischen Theaters,:" trans., John Willett in *Brecht on Theatre* 123.

19 Bertolt Brecht, "Kurze Beschreibung einer neuen Technik der Schauspielkunst, die einen Verfremdungseffekt hervorbringt," trans., John Willett in *Brecht on Theatre* 145.

20 Edward Bond, taped correspondence, January 1982.

21 Edward Bond, "A Note on Dramatic Method" in *The Bundle* (London: Methuen, 1978) xvii.

22 Bond, "A Note on Dramatic Method," xvii/iii.

23 Edward Bond, personal interview, 14 December 1989.

24 Wanda Rulewicz, *A Semiotic Study of the Plays of Edward Bond* (Warsaw: Wydawnictaw Uniwesytetu Warszawskiego, 1987)

25 Edward Bond, personal interview, 12 June 1990.

26 David L. Hirst, *Edward Bond* (London: Macmillan, 1985) 155/6.

27 Edward Bond, letter to author, 22 April 1990.

28 Edward Bond, "Notes on Theatre Events," 11 January 1990.

29 Edward Bond, personal interview, 12 June 1990.

30 Edward Bond, personal interview, 12 June 1990.

31 Edward Bond, personal interview, 12 June 1990.

32 Edward Bond, "Commentary on 'The War Plays.'" *The War Plays* (London: Methuen, 1991) 317.

33 Edward Bond, personal interview, 22 December 1991.

34 Edward Bond, interview with Nick Philippou, undated.

35 Philip Davis, personal interview, 29 January 1990.

36 Edward Bond, personal interview, 12 June 1990.

37 Edward Bond, letter to James Holloway, 1 December 1990.

38 Edward Bond, taped correspondence, January 1982.

Chapter One

The Woman

Edward Bond made his British directorial debut with the open-ing of *The Woman* on August 10, 1978 on the Olivier stage of Britain's National Theatre. It was the first new play to be pro-duced in the Olivier. Although the decision to direct his own work had been met with a mixed reaction from the critics, the majority praised Bond's handling of this complex large-scale drama. Martin Esslin wrote in *Plays and Players*:

> The Olivier was planned to accommodate the large-scale classical drama: there are few contemporary plays, and even fewer contempo-rary playwrights, capable of competing with works conceived on such a scale. It is a measure of Edward Bond's stature as a playwright that his new play seems entirely appropriate to the stage.[1]

The influence on Bond of this huge 1160 seat semi-circular the-atre cannot easily be dismissed. Contrary to claims by Peter Lewis, the National Theatre did not commission *The Woman* although Bond has stated that a description of the Olivier audi-torium from a newspaper was in the "back of his mind" as he wrote the play.[2] Peter Hall, then director of the National The-atre, observed that the Olivier was a test for Bond:

> The landmark as far as *The Woman* was concerned was that it brought the drama onto the Olivier stage and showed that people like Edward Bond could go the distance in a big space.[3]

Bond's decision to use the stage of the Olivier when approached by the National Theatre, caused Peter Hall some administrative difficulties as he relates in his diaries:

Wednesday 26 October 1977
A talk with Edward Bond which I believed I mishandled. I told him we couldn't do his new play *The Woman* in the Olivier until next autumn,

but we could do it in the Cottesloe in the spring. He said he would
have to consider his position, but the clear implication was he was
withdrawing the play. What did I do wrong? Well, I did mention that
we had to play to 80% in the Olivier, and as a consequence he gave me
a short talk about the wickedness of the National Theatre having to be
commercial. I asked him to tell that to the Board and the Arts
Council.[4]

Bond waited until Autumn 1978 to stage *The Woman* in the
Olivier. Certainly if the play was not written with the resources
of the Olivier in mind, Bond discovered during rehearsals that
this theatre was an ideal forum for the play. In an article entitled *Us, Our Drama and the National Theatre*, Bond described the
Olivier as a public place, "where history is formed, classes clash
and whole societies move":

> The Olivier stage is ideally suited to this sort of theatre. It's like a pub-
> lic square for the meeting of several roads or a playing field or a factory
> floor or a place of assembly and debate.[5]

As well as his revolutionary use of the stage, which by all the
written accounts was remarkable, the main factor behind
Bond's decision to direct his own work was that in the Olivier
he saw a theatre "that can help us to create the new sort of acting we need to demonstrate our world to audiences."[6] He
maintains that with *The Woman*, "I've reached a position where
I'm making new demands on actors in my writing. I have to
interpret the making of these demands."[7]

Ideas for a work based on the Trojan Wars date back to 1973.
According to Malcolm Hay and Philip Roberts, Bond's play *The
Fool* interrupted the writing process, which did not get under
way again until February of the following year.[8] By June of 1975
he put aside *The Woman* for one more year in order to write a
number of short plays, not completing it until 1977.

In *The Woman*, Bond plunders the myths found in Homer
and Euripides and echoes Sophocles' *Antigone*, *Oedipus Rex*, and
Philoctetes, re-working classical sources to demonstrate what he
considers the injustices of our present society. But why does
Bond turn to ancient Greek events in order to describe the present? James C. Bulman states in an article on the play:

All Bond's favorite themes are here: the wrongful view of man as a depraved animal, the senselessness of violence, the disease of tyranny, the inevitable fall of a society which exploits the working class.[9]

The Woman is subtitled "Scenes of War and Freedom." As Ruby Cohn has indicated, this helps divide the play into two sections: Part One revolving around the Trojan War, Part Two occurring twelve years later on the island where both Hecuba and Ismene experience relative freedom.[10]

Part One is Bond's version of Homer's *Iliad*. As in Homer, the Greeks attack Troy, but here not in an attempt to reclaim Helen. Instead they want the stone goddess of Good Fortune, a statue that represents mankind's belief in superhuman powers. Occupying Helen's place in the myth, the statue is an objectified representation of a woman and is both a symbol of good and evil. The goddess may even be the woman of the play's title. Hecuba treats the stone with contempt, recognizing it only as a source of her and her peoples' problems, but Heros, the Greek commander, believes totally in the power of the goddess to change his destiny. Such commitment to his belief drives Heros forward, blinding him to the suffering that the belief will cause others. Once Priam, King of Troy, is dead and power has transferred not to his son but his wife Hecuba, the Greeks send Thersites and Ismene, wife of Heros, to acquire the statue, assuring Hecuba that in return they will offer peace. But Hecuba, suspecting that the Greeks will still attack her city once they have the statue, refuses, accepting instead Ismene's offer to stay in Troy as her hostage. Ismene's suggestion can be seen as an expression of her growing independence and realization about the hollowness of Greek promises. A take-over occurs in Troy, and Hecuba's son replaces Hecuba as leader. Despite Ismene's plea to the Greeks not to attack Troy, soldiers continue to advance. With the outbreak of plague in Troy and now the threat of death upon them, the Trojan people kill Hecuba's son and throw the statue of the goddess out of the city. As Hecuba had prophesied, her city is ransacked and burnt. In a scene reminiscent of the anarchic violence ending Act One of Bond's *Lear*, Ismene, like Antigone in Sophocles's play, is walled up to die and many Trojans are murdered, including

Astyanax, Hecuba's young grandson, whom Heros orders thrown from the city walls. Hecuba, not wishing to witness Astyanax's death, and as a defiant gesture against the Greeks, blinds herself in one eye, leaving the other eye intact to enable her to see Heros's reaction. Part One closes with silence as soldiers tap on the wall in which Ismene is entombed.

Part Two opens twelve years later on an island reminiscent of the pastoral, golden-age world often found in Bond's plays. Hecuba has chosen to blind herself totally with the aid of a plug and band placed over her surviving eye. She is led by Ismene who, having "lost her mind," has been rescued from the walls of Troy by soldiers seeking the wealth buried with her. Nestor, an ageing Greek statesman, visits them to entice Hecuba to Greece and locate the statue. "It's gone," Hecuba reports, describing the statue's fate at sea during a storm. Part Two also sees the arrival of the Dark Man, seeking refuge on the island from the Athenian silver mines. Falling in love with Ismene, the Dark Man is given asylum and permitted to stay. Heros, personally supervising the sea's division into areas to search for the statue, gives the Dark Man a pardon. This action fails to bring him any closer to Hecuba, Heros's intention, nor are his romantic advances towards Ismene, his former wife, successful. Nestor's arrival to order Heros back to Athens prompts Hecuba to invent her dream: the goddess is ready to leave the sea and her whereabouts will be revealed to the winner of a race run between Heros and the crippled Dark Man. The victor of this race must kill the loser. Heros wins, but the Dark Man, in league with Hecuba, kills him. Having obtained revenge, Hecuba is killed by a tornado, leaving Ismene and the Dark Man, like Willy and Rose at the end of *The Sea* or David and Ann at the end of *Summer*, to create their future together.

With *The Woman*, Bond only uses a classical framework as an opening into a set of familiar themes. "A Socialist Rhapsody," published in 1980 with the text of the play, contains Bond's view on *The Woman* and an explanation as to why he is selective in the myths that he uses:

> In *The Woman* I ignore many things because I wish to make clear both
> the point of the story (that history is a moral force, that morality gets

its meaning from human beings and that our actions can have morally good results) and my reason for telling it (to celebrate the world and people of which these things are true.)[11]

Bond's plays aim at contemporary social comment by using history as a vehicle for exploring present-day society, whether the setting is the world of Greek myth, the seventeenth century landscape of *Bingo*, cities of the present in *Jackets II*, or those of the future, as in *The War Plays*. Examining the principal characters in *The Woman*, Hecuba and Ismene, and briefly discussing the dramatic function of Heros and the Dark Man, it will be possible to demonstrate how Bond uses an ancient tale to describe a situation as relevant to our society as it would be to the audience of the original myth.

An audience "see" Hecuba first through Heros's eyes. Presented as "an old aristocratic whore," she appears power-hungry and stubborn, unwilling to give into the Greeks.[12] This image contrasts with her actual appearance in scene four as a "dignified public figure," prepared to do anything to avert the death of innocent people.[13] At the time of the production of *The Woman*, Bond referred to Hecuba as a female version of Lear.[14] This idea is reflected in the play's first part. Until scene seven, Hecuba is exposed to the brutalities and pointlessness of war. She remarks to Ismene: "If men were sensible they wouldn't have to go to war."[15] Her withdrawal from society is apparent in scene seven at the prison. Hecuba now appears as a deposed leader under house arrest resigned to the destruction of Troy. Scene fourteen sees Hecuba take action, not against the system but against herself, by ripping out her eye.

Part Two offers Hecuba an opportunity for retreat. With Ismene to guide her, she enjoys the quiet of the island:

> I love to play on the beach, there's nothing to bump into—O not running and horseplay, losing your breath at my age isn't a pleasure—but walk on the sand and let the water-line guide me. I listen to the sea and it washes away all my anger and so I'm at peace.[16]

Yet the sea is a corrosive force and catalyst for change in the play. As with water images in *The Sea* and *Summer*, stillness masks the chaos underneath—the sea which exhumes Colin's dead body in *The Sea* and the war dead of *Summer*. In *The*

Woman the sea appears soothing but actually contains the statue and carries Heros and his soldiers to the island. Like Lear, who craves the comfort of Thomas's and Susan's house, and Shakespeare hiding in his garden in *Bingo*, Hecuba has no desire to confront the cause of Troy's undoing, a way of life represented by the Greeks. But the arrival of Nestor, the Dark Man and Heros threatens her existence. Hecuba's response is not to defend herself but to detect the cause for her suffering and rationally eliminate it. In this sense, her final action against Heros, conspiring in his death, is similar to Lear's gesture at the end of Bond's play, symbolic of an audience's need to radically alter the way society is constructed. In this action and the survival of Ismene, the Dark Man and the islanders lies Bond's hope for the future:

> Their situation can be compared to an African state that is thrown into the twentieth century after a period of colonial occupation. . . One should feel that the islanders, Ismene and the Dark Man will organize themselves.[17]

Ruby Cohn is the only critic to suggest that the play's title may not refer to Hecuba but Ismene.[18] Although Cohn does not explain her rationale it may be based on the fact that, like Hecuba, Ismene undergoes a transformation during the play. In Part One, she becomes convinced of Troy's need for reassurance that the Greeks will not attack them. This results in her choosing to stay in Troy, subsequently telling Thersites that she will remain in the enemy camp to ensure no military attack is carried out by the Greeks. The conclusion of Part One sees Ismene shouting to Greek soldiers to return home and being enclosed within the wall for her traitorous behavior. Between Parts One and Two, Ismene suffers amnesia and regresses to a child-like state where her prime function is to act as Hecuba's slave, "an animal who gets two meals a day for being house trained and taking you round on a lead."[19] Bond has stated that Ismene has to lose her sanity in the second half of the play:

> [In the first half] Ismene *could* be said to be mad because her reason is non-effective in that society. So in the second half I made her mad because she has all this practical understanding and it is of no practical use.[20]

A significant change to Ismene occurs with the arrival of the Dark Man. As symbolized in the "tickling scene," this character liberates Ismene, helping to redefine and rebuild her life on more solid, rational principles. Ultimately, this results in Ismene's mind being restored, and together she and the Dark Man can face the future. As she remarks: "Since you've loved me my mind's begun to clear."[21]

Ismene's child-like quality is shared throughout the play by Heros, his moods swinging from acting the responsible commander, to pleading with Ismene in Part Two, scene five, to know the statue's whereabouts. Nestor indulges Heros in his actions which suggest a child-like spontaneity: walling up Ismene at the end of Part One, his killing of Astyanax in triumph at Troy's destruction, and his sexual advances toward Ismene in Part Two. Most child-like is searching for "a little stone in the sea."[22] As David L. Hirst indicates in his book on Bond, Heros's relentlessness over finding the goddess "powerfully emphasizes the folly of the politician desperately attempting to make his power secure."[23] This incident reveals Bond's attempt at exposing the pointlessness of the Trojan War, and, by extension, any war. The play demonstrates that leaders cannot be satisfied whilst there lurks the possibility of a threat. The Dark Man comments on the stupidity of men's actions: "They catch netfuls of fish and tip them back into the sea. If fish could think they'd say men were mad."[24] This striking image of foolishness resonates in an age which produces and wastes goods and services which cannot be sold for profit, while others starve.

Free Man, written by Bond for Paul Freeman, the actor playing the Dark Man at the Olivier, is a story containing the background to the Dark Man's arrival on the island.[25] It raises a question as to why the Dark Man fled the grim conditions of the Athenian silver mines, rather than choosing suicide. The answer lies in the Man's faith to take risks—a characteristic shared by Hecuba. As she ponders her decision to obtain his pardon for escaping, the Dark Man gradually realizes that Hecuba has attributes he respects: personal integrity and belief in an individual's strength. Hecuba also recognizes these qualities in the Dark Man. For example, she remarks: "In your mind you were as safe as a mouse in its hole. . . O you'd have lived a few more years. Rats don't last long once they scuttle out to the light."[26] But Hecuba understands the issue of Heros's responsibility much more clearly than the Dark Man:

> It was clear when that smiling old man came and said 'statue' that one day this island would be pulled out of the sea by its roots and the people on it shaken down like ants. He [Heros] should be killed.[27]

By appealing to his own experience in the mine, Hecuba gradually persuades the Man that Heros must be killed and he must be the murderer. Like Hecuba and Ismene, the Man is also disabled, possibly from working in the mines or perhaps from birth. What is significant about this deformity is his ability to transform it into a strength that ultimately conquers Heros.

The production of *The Woman* gave rise to a series of fundamental questions regarding the nature of the acting style needed for the play's presentation. By his own testimony, Bond's predominant concerns with acting were the application of emotion avoiding a "naturalistic" acting style and the release of an "athletic" energy, which, according to Bond, should be an actor's emotional storing house.[28] Each of these stylistic elements will be explored. At times Bond appears to make contradictory statements about the acting style required for his plays, mixing intellectual approaches with physical imagistic techniques. However, I believe Bond's comments reflect those of a director searching for definitions of his work in practice.

As already noted, the auditorium's size itself played a role in establishing a style. In an article which appeared at the time of *The Woman*, Bond emphasized the demands of the Olivier which indicated that a different acting style be adopted:

> [the weakness of method acting] often passes unnoticed because it is seen close to, where it can overwhelm usually because of its primitive force. On the Olivier it is seen for what it is: not just right acting in the wrong place, but a lie. A lie because it cannot tell a story.[29]

According to Bond, an actor who brings only an emotional charge to his work is obsessed: "People who surrender themselves to obsessions go to madhouses. Our acting must not be an obsession with the past. It is directed to the future."[30]

A central characteristic of Bond's drama in performance is the energy required of an actor. Bond draws a distinction between the "frenzied" energy of musical theatre and what is demanded by his work:

> We don't want the abstract energy of American musicals . . . the bombast of the old actors . . . the medical twitch of method acting. . . Our acting does not recreate. It recollects. Its energy is intellectual. It makes the particular general and the general particular. It finds the law in the incidental. Thus it restores the moral importance to human behaviour.[31]

The style that developed was expressed through Bond's use of private/public images in the text. In later plays these images were used consciously to form the TE. An example of a private/public incident can be found in Part One, scene two, between Heros and Ismene. Set in Heros's quarters, it could be an intimate scene, but Bond does not use this occasion simply to build character. Bond has remarked:

> In this play what I wanted to do was to say, "Look I want a scene in the courtroom and a scene in the bedroom." I want the strong consciousness of domestic people, but I wanted the organisation of the church, the community. I wanted to contrast the private and public and show they are absolutely one.[32]

Ismene's concern is that Heros will not keep his word and will still attack Troy. As he indicates by his vision of the imagined incident inside the Trojan camp of scene one, Heros is obsessed with Hecuba. He sees the Trojan leader as a threat to order of the state that he will one day dictate. Bond's notion of forcing a character's privacy into the wider socio-political arena is understood by Nick Philippou, a director of Bond's work. Philippou develops Bond's idea of making the private public by distinguishing between a psychological approach to acting and Bond's theories:

> Stanislavsky mentions "given circumstances." I think Bond would talk about them too but he would suggest they were slightly different: given *social* circumstances rather than given *personal* circumstances.[33]

Philippou suggests that Stanislavsky is able, at least in part, to regard the individual outside his social context, something Bond is unable to do.

The creation of images and an audience's connection with them during performance, is a hallmark of Bond's theatre. These signals carried by the play became known in 1986 as TEs as Bond consciously used them (and so described them) in his plays. Bond's rehearsal process is the opportunity for an actor's discovery of TEs. Examples can be given from Bond's production of *The Woman* which demonstrate the actor's discovery of these moments and indicate the importance of such images to Bond's theory of theatre.[34]

An account of the production states that significant images were created at the beginning of Part One, scene five, as Heros obtained the statue but lost his wife:

> Heros stood, hunched, with his chin resting in the palm of one hand, physically and emotionally wrapped in himself not knowing what to do; not a god, as he half suggested in scene two, but a little boy. As the short scene with Nestor began, Heros snapped out of this stance and his attitude became something very different—his expression now not glowering but neutral, as he asked Nestor business-like questions about the danger of Ismene's position.[35]

By capturing in this one image the complexity of the character and allowing an audience to see how Heros is physically changed by social circumstance, Bond created a TE. Another example of a TE is the limp of the Dark Man. The play describes him as "deformed," however Bond discovered that it might assist an audience if his limp "disappeared" as he recognized Hecuba's goodness but returned as he faced Heros.[36] This formed a TE in that Bond hoped this action might suggest that Hecuba's path leads to social understanding and development whereas Heros's understanding of the world would only create a destruction. These moments contain the essence of Bond's notion of a TE. By transferring his political and theoretical understanding of a character into theatrical terms, Bond fulfills what he considers the dual purpose of a TE:

> One, what incident will be chosen to show something (examples, putting on a dress, sitting on a chair, spitting). Two, how the incident

is acted—how do you spit, sit, talk etc.—which will display the meaning of the character in the incident.[37]

Heros's gesture, as he challenged anyone to race with him, was also developed as a TE. Nicky Henson, playing Heros in Bond's production, had his "legs spread, arms flung wide, head thrown back."[38] This image provided a TE by capturing the arrogant spirit of triumph that can be associated with this character. Unlike Delsarte's table of physical gestures, Bond's TE aims to capture the play's intellectual and political dynamic and then conjure the appropriate emotions from an audience.[39] Consequently, an audience is not manipulated by artificial feelings but those emotions which arise directly out of the play's political situation.

A further example of a TE, although not created consciously as such, was the image Bond designed as the Greeks arrived on the island:

> [The islanders] ran up and disappeared off the end of the stage. Vanished. So the Greeks were all alone. Slowly I made the heads come up so the whole thing was like a ring of beads. I wanted to hold that for quite some time because I wanted them to think the heads were all chopped off. . . I like this idea because the moment before you had seen them dancing. Suddenly this army arrived and they were reduced to their heads. They had got to think, they never thought outside their normal thought process. It was very exciting seeing this ring of heads, it was also like the audience.[40]

Perhaps the most significant image in the play was that of the crowd in Part One, scene twelve and Part Two. Both are based on different responses to a similar cause. In scene twelve the people of Troy are united by fear, a feeling Bond captures with the gesture of their hands, but in Part Two the islanders' expressions of resentment at the Greeks' arrival are more individualistic. Bond discusses his approach in scene twelve:

> A crowd of poor people force some rich people to back up a flight of steps and then takes [sic] a statue from a temple. I tried to show their common purpose through their hands. First their hands are flat and extended, the hands of beggars; when they come close to their enemies their hands become fists; when they carry out the statue their hands are weapons, claws and flails; and when they're united in one moment of choice (to give the statue to the Greeks) their hands swing in the direction of the harbour like the leaves of a tree turning in the wind.[41]

The importance of the hand movement is described in Bond's poems "Hands." This poem traces the change of the gesture, from hands that "are as flat and open as empty plates," to hands that "swing in one common direction."[42] Bond indicates that the actors' approach differed in Part Two; they gave each of the islanders an individual quality:

> An island occupied by foreign troops. In rehearsals the actors discussed the ways in which they could react. Some wanted to resist, others to quietly comply because they saw their situation as hopeless. Of those who wanted to resist, some wanted guerilla action and others wanted an open attack, because guerilla action would provoke reprisals. All these reactions are recorded in performance.[43]

As the director, Bond received conflicting criticism for his approach, some critics wanting "picturesque individuals" in scene twelve and a crowd with a united purpose in Part Two.[44]

Bond also created sound images. These were not meant to provide moments of social insight like TEs, but rather augment the play's intellectual arguments by connecting otherwise disassociated moments and assisting an audience in forming links between incidents. Timothy Norton, who played Astyanax at the National Theatre, observed one moment of imagistic association crucial to Bond's form of theatre:

> [Bond] was concerned with even the smallest and simplest effects. There's one scene with a priest talking about the entrails of a dove and Bond got one actor, sitting there with a drum, going "bang-bang-bang." Sitting there, drumming all the way through the scene. *He used that at another point, too.* (my emphasis).[45]

In his essay, "Working from 'Up Here,'" David Jansen indicates that Bond wanted his production of *The Woman* to be "choreographed carefully in terms of movement, sound and gesture."[46] By arranging the production's physical elements, Bond was able to "shift the actor's emphasis from the personal to the social."[47] Bond's notion of images can be seen as similar to the strategy of Brecht and his concept of "gestus." In his *Short Organum for the Theatre*, Brecht defines this idea:

> The realm of attitudes adopted by the characters towards one another is what we call the realm of gest. Physical attitude, tone of voice and

facial expression are all determined by a social gest: the characters are cursing, flattering, instructing one another and so on. The attitudes which people adopt towards one another include even those attitudes which would appear to be quite private, such as the utterances of physical pain in an illness, or of religious faith. These expressions of a gest are usually highly complicated and contradictory, so that they cannot be rendered by any single word and the actor must take care that in giving his image the necessary emphasis he does not lose anything, but emphasizes the entire complex.[48]

Whereas the Brechtian "gestus" can refer directly to society as a whole, the Bondian "gestus," or TE, refers to the dramatic world of the play occurring inside the theatre. I do not mean to imply Bond's theories have no application outside their dramatic surroundings. On the contrary Bond maintains that, as a result of TEs, wider implications are felt by an audience. However, as their name suggests, initially TEs operate only in the theatre by illuminating and crystallizing a character or situation. Bond expands on his theoretical distinction between Brecht's concept of "gestus" and the TE:

Brecht's theory . . . [does] not abstract in the way he suggests. The famous example of the street accident where they all stand around and say this happened and that happened. They don't. One is a dedicated pedestrian and thinks that all motorists are mad anyway. Another is a racing driver fanatic and thinks the whole problem with cities is that people are allowed to walk in them. Someone else dislikes grey hair. There is no way of making an audience abstract their experiences. What you have to do is engage an audience. . . Estrangement is a negative and I think the theatre is always engaged in the particular. What you are doing to the idea of alienation is changing it by saying, "Yes, but what does society use theatre for?" In that way there is no external guarantee.[49]

Michael Chekhov's "psychological gesture" is a technique to assist the actor in finding the emotional essence of his character. Nick Philippou believes that Michael Chekhov's approach is less helpful than Bond's TE as it makes the play "live" only for the actor not an audience:

What I think Bond asks an actor to do is play the breadth of the character's experience in the play as the experience of many people which connects with Bond's feeling of the contradictory nature of human experience.[50]

As a director, Bond is more concerned than other theoreticians, such as Michael Chekhov, with the wider implications of
his theory for an audience: "I am not interested in what an
audience says when it leaves the theatre, but I am interested in
what it would say about the play it had seen six months afterwards."[51] For Bond, it is in the theatre that questions about
how political power is distributed need to be asked and tenta-
tive solutions provided. To achieve this, Bond believes full theatrical resources should be made available. In his production of
The Woman, it became clear that what appeared complex on the
page can be explicated in the theatre with, among other things,
visual elements.

Bond and the designer, Hayden Griffin, literally stripped the
stage of the Olivier theatre, exposing the fire screen not normally seen by the public. This screen had been painted black
but, after the paint had been removed, revealed a wall of silver.
Griffin commented on this design element:

> The important thing to make clear is that it was Edward's idea to open
> the stage right to the back. The silver doors on the Olivier stage came
> from *The Woman* because when we came in those doors were painted
> black. It was Edward's idea to combine this mechanical effect with this
> romantic landscape. So we scraped the paint off the door which Dexter
> and Peter Hall then used for *Galileo*. The biggest expense on *The
> Woman* was these people rubbing all the paint off these doors.[52]

The doors served as an important component in the play's
action, rising halfway at the end of Part One to represent the
ruined wall of Troy. Fire and smoke billowed from the side fur-
thest away from the audience to indicate what one critic
described as, the "holocaust inside."[53] Part Two occurred on a
large tilted disc representing the island with Hecuba's hut stage
right and a few silver boulders stage left. The silver wall was
present throughout lit to suggest an "endless horizon of sea and
sky surrounding the island."[54] There were no other scenic elements with the exception of a large red cloth for Part One that
covered the stage representing the bloodshed of the Trojan
wars. The use of this cloth prompted Bond to write "On The
Red Floor Covering," a short poem capturing the social distinction between the actors and those who "walk before us on a red
carpet."[55]

As with Bond's subsequent productions, the lighting alternately bathed the stage in a bright white light and illuminated areas for the short scenes. Also consistent with Bond's later directing style, the intensity of the lighting was increased during the scene changes, demystifying the theatrical experience for an audience and emphasizing that they were in the theatre watching a play. This harsh light and absence of substantial pieces of scenery emphasized the size of the Olivier stage, a space that Bond fully utilized.

The storm was an important effect in Part Two, scene seven, causing one critic to remark that it was the most "resonant thunder I ever felt in the theater."[56] Bond recalls this effect as an example of the play's austerity:

> I remember the storm. I wanted this to be very, very frightening. I wanted very much for Bryceland [Hecuba] to be left alone on stage and just walk up the ramp of the stage and at the end she would just look into the storm, a bit like a ship's head, the wind was an image of historical change. If you contrast that moment when she discovers she is blind (she came down to the other end of the stage, right in the lap of the audience and lit this little tiny candle) . . . and then striding around in this storm then I think you can see the extremes through which the play moves.[57]

But the tempest was more than simply a stage effect as a writer about Bond has observed. Margaret Biddle, a commentator on Bond's production work, interpreted the storm as a significant image working on both the literary and metaphorical levels. Biddle argues that on the occasions a storm occurs, between Part One and Two and in Part Two, scene six, seven and eight, they consistently represent "great social upheaval."[58] To this should be added the storm's ability to claim lives: the death of those in the shipwreck and finally the death of Hecuba.

Bond recorded two incidents from rehearsals which he shared with the audience through some poems in the program. The first poem, entitled "Astyanax," reveals how the actors playing Cassandra, Hecuba and Ismene rehearsed using a cardboard box instead of the young actor playing Astyanax. Evidently this was because the actors and Bond did not want to frighten the child. The fragility with which the women held the box for fear of crushing it, provided Bond with the perfect metaphor for one of the play's ideas. The last lines of the poem confront us with the main issue:

> So the child is taken
>
> How can we change the world
> With tenderness.[59]

Bond saw the contradiction of those like Heros who would kill the innocent boy and the careful handling of the box by the three women who were afraid of hurting the child. "A Stage Direction" explains how the literalness of the make-up crew from *The Woman* shocked Bond into considering an analogy between the plague-ridden women of Troy and society's diseases. As with much of his work, Bond's poems capture the essence of his dialectic by joining the play's issues to their universal consequences.

In his diaries, Peter Hall provides an account of a working relationship with Bond. From the beginning, Hall seems to have assumed that difficulties with Bond were going to arise.

> Friday 21 July 1978
> [Bond] was open to suggestion; no problem at all. I am optimistic. Great relief for *I had been expecting a terrible crisis*.[60] (my emphasis)

Despite his personal concerns about Bond, Hall concludes that the production was "magnificently staged" and a "superb play."[61] However, in his accounts of the production, Hall made no attempt at charting the progress of Bond's "alternative" approach to acting. The failure at creating an acting style was to result in Bond's own disillusion with the production and abandonment of the professional theatre for three years. This approach to acting, and how it shaped the production process, must be established if Bond's development as a director is going to be studied.

Nicky Henson, playing Heros in Bond's production, had difficulties in understanding Bond's approach. Henson's impression was that Bond required an unemotive technique. Accord-

ing to Henson, Bond made it very clear that "Victorian/ emo-
tional/sentimental acting," was unacceptable. Although he
wanted a different method, Henson felt that Bond could not
explain what it was:

> What we would do is interpretive acting and he did not want us to
> interpret his words, just speak them. How does an actor do this, like an
> automaton and an audience just sit there and listen and, ironically,
> make their own interpretation of the work?[62]

Henson's problem in understanding Bond's approach as a
director was shared by many actors who worked on this and
subsequent plays which Bond directed. A possible explanation
for an actor's confusion is that Bond clearly challenges per-
formers, asking them to think in a way not required by a drama
school training.

Bond's struggle to create an alternative approach to acting is
perhaps best understood by Daniel Baron Cohen. Cohen was a
very close associate of Bond's, acting as assistant director on
Nick Hamm's production of *The Worlds* and working with Bond
on *Restoration* at the Royal Court and *Summer* at the National
Theatre:

> [Bond] was trying to create a socialist realism, the right gestures. Some
> actors become very insecure and frustrated and communication
> becomes tense when actors are thrown on their own resources. . .
> Edward also wants to lose pomposity and ornamentation but I don't
> think actors feel secure with the simplicity Edward is after.[63]

Margaret Ford appeared in Bond's production of *The Woman* in
two roles: as one of the three Trojan women with the plague,
and Rossa. In 1989, Ford worked with Bond again when she
acted the part of Mrs Lewis in the touring production of *Jackets*.
She echoes Cohen's comments about simplicity, adding: "The
point is with Edward, he keeps on breaking stuff down until the
bitter end and maybe that is where there are problems with
actors."[64] By this, Ford seems to suggest that Bond distills an
actor's approach to his character down to its essential social
characteristics. Yvonne Bryceland, playing Hecuba, described
how she needed to surrender herself intellectually but not emotionally:

> The only way I could work with him [Bond] was to say that intellectu-
> ally I am at your mercy but emotionally . . . maybe I have an instinctive
> response.[65]

Bryceland was convinced that Bond should direct the first production of his own plays and felt that without Bond present she
would have been unable to work:

> There are certain kinds of actors who respond to him whole-heartedly
> and Edward gets splendid work out of them. He got terrific work out
> of some of the actors in *The Woman*, so much so that people still talk
> about aspects of that production and I think how can people say that
> he cannot direct his own work when this is a production they will
> always remember?[66]

The particular qualities of Bryceland as an actor will be further
explored when she worked with Bond on *Summer* in 1982.
However, Bryceland emphasized in connection with *The
Woman* the difficulty she had in analyzing her own acting style
in relation to Bond's plays:

> [My acting style] is very hard to describe. It's not like going into a
> dream because one has always got a percentage of one's brain in touch
> with the audience. I can't take my performance apart and examine it
> because I don't work like that.[67]

In Bryceland's opinion, what is needed in Bond's form of
theatre are actors gifted with patience prepared to confront
their own class position. According to Bryceland, ideological
compatibility was not a requirement, although it may assist in
the creative process:

> You do not *have* to be of any political persuasion, maybe it helps but I
> just think it relates to a certain generosity, understanding and caring
> about the issues Edward writes on. It is the human being Edward writes
> about.[68]

After *The Woman*, Bond went on to direct the first two productions, and assist on a third, of a new play written during his
residence as Northern Arts Literary Fellow, entitled *The Worlds*.
Following his experience at the National Theatre, Bond abandoned the professional theatre turning instead to university
students and the academic world for inspiration. Although
Bond was to discover a mixture of talent in Newcastle and Lon-

don where the play was performed, it was undoubtedly a relief to exchange the rigors of professional theatre for the comparatively relaxed atmosphere of student theatre where some experimentation could take place. Bond did not return to the professional arena until 1981 with his production of *Restoration* at the Royal Court Theatre in London.

Notes

1 Martin Esslin, "The Woman," *Plays and Players* 26 (1) October 1978: 26.

2 Peter Lewis, *The National–A Dream Made Concrete* (London: Methuen, 1990) 135 "*The Woman* was the first play to be written specifically for the Olivier stage." Edward Bond, draft article for *Socialist Challenge*, August 1978 quoted in *Bond: A Study of his Plays* by Malcolm Hay and Philip Roberts (London: Methuen, 1980) 239.

3 Peter Hall, personal interview, 17 July 1990.

4 Peter Hall, *Peter Hall's Diaries—The Story of a Dramatic Battle* ed. John Goodwin (London: Hamish Hamilton, 1984) 318/9.

5 Edward Bond in "Us, Our Drama and the National Theatre." *Plays and Players* 26 (1) October 1978: 8.

6 Bond, "Us, Our Drama and the National Theatre:" 9.

7 Bond, draft article for *Socialist Challenge*.

8 Malcolm Hay and Philip Roberts in *Bond: A Study of his Plays* 238.

9 James C. Bulman, "'The Woman' and Greek Myth: Bond's Theatre of History." *Modern Drama* 29 (4) 1986: 506/7.

10 Ruby Cohn, "The Fabulous Theater of Edward Bond." *Essays on Contemporary British Drama* (Munich: Hueber, 1981) 200/1.

11 Edward Bond, "A Socialist Rhapsody." *Bond Plays: Three* (London: Methuen, 1987) 269/70.

12 Bond, "The Woman" appears in *Plays: Three* 176.

13 Bond, *The Woman* 186.

14 Bond quoted in *Observer* (Sunday Plus) 15 January 1978: 31.

15 Bond, *The Woman* 191.

16 Bond, *The Woman* 232.

17 Edward Bond, personal interview, 12 June 1990.

18 Cohn, "The Fabulous Theater of Edward Bond" 202.

19 Bond, *The Woman* 241.

20 Edward Bond, personal interview, 12 June 1990.

21 Bond, *The Woman* 268.

22 Bond, *The Woman* 266.

23 David L. Hirst, *Edward Bond* (London: Macmillan, 1985) 64.

24 Bond, *The Woman* 245.

25 "Free Man" is reprinted in *Bond: Plays Three* 298-302.

26 Bond, *The Woman*, 236.

27 Bond, *The Woman* 252.

28 Edward Bond, "Creating what is Normal," by Tony Coult *Plays and Players* December 1975: 12.

29 Bond, "Us, Our Drama and the National Theatre:" 9.

30 Bond, "Notes on Acting 'The Woman'" in *Bond: Plays Three* 287.

31 Bond, "Notes on Acting 'The Woman'" 288.

32 Edward Bond, personal interview, 12 June 1990.

33 Nick Philippou, personal interview, 15 December 1989.

34 I am grateful to Malcolm Hay and Philip Roberts who provide a detailed account of Bond's production of *The Woman* in *Bond: A Study of his Plays*.

35 *Bond: A Study of his Plays* 252.

36 *Bond: A Study of his Plays* 259.

37 Edward Bond, letter to author, 8 October 1990.

38 *Bond: A Study of his Plays* 261.

39 Delsarte's work is explained briefly in footnote 10 of the Introduction.

40 Edward Bond, personal interview, 12 June 1990.

41 Bond, "Us, Our Drama and the National Theatre:" 9.

42 Edward Bond, "Hands" reprinted in *Bond Plays: Three* 289/90.

43 Bond, "Us, Our Drama and the National Theatre:" 9.

44 Bond, "Us, Our Drama and the National Theatre:" 9.

45 Timothy Norton quoted by David Jansen, "Working from 'Up Here,'" diss. Royal Holloway and Bedford New College, May 1989, 8.

46 Jansen 8.

47 Hirst 43.

48 Bertolt Brecht, "A Short Organum for the Theatre," from 'Sinn und Form,' Sonderheft Bertolt Brecht, Potsdam, 1949 in *Brecht on Theatre* trans., John Willett, (London: Methuen, 1974) 198.

49 Edward Bond, personal interview, 12 June 1990.

50 Nick Philippou, personal interview, 15 December 1989.

51 Edward Bond, letter to author, November 1983.

52 Hayden Griffin, personal interview, 21 February 1990.

53 B. A. Young, "The Woman," *Financial Times* 11 August 1978.

54 *Bond: A Study of his Plays* 242.

55 Edward Bond, "On The Red Floor Covering." *Bond: Plays Three* 275.

56 Cohn, *The Fabulous Theater of Edward Bond* 203.

57 Edward Bond, personal interview, 12 June 1990.

58 Margaret Biddle, "Learning and Teaching for Change and The Plays of Edward Bond," diss. University of York, October 1985, 81.

59 Edward Bond, "Astynax," *Bond Plays: Three* 274.

60 Hall *Diaries* 365/6.

61 Hall *Diaries* 365 and 368.

62 Nicky Henson, personal interview, 6 June 1990.

63 Daniel Baron Cohen, personal interview, 16 June 1990.

64 Margaret Ford, personal interview, 16 October 1989.

65 Yvonne Bryceland, telephone interview, 3 December 1989.

66 Yvonne Bryceland, telephone interview, 3 December 1989.

67 Yvonne Bryceland, telephone interview, 23 June 1990.

68 Yvonne Bryceland, telephone interview, 23 June 1990.

Chapter Two

The Worlds

The Worlds was written during Bond's appointment in 1977/79 as Northern Arts Literary Fellow in the universities of Newcastle and Durham along with "The Activists Papers," a series of essays and poems covering the period 1978-80. These serve as an introduction to, and examination of, the play and its implications. Its first production, by students at Newcastle Playhouse, took place on March 8, 1979. *The Worlds* was subsequently performed at the Royal Court Theatre Upstairs in London, by the Theatre's Activists Youth Theatre Club on November 21, 1979. A new professional production came two years later, at the New Half Moon Theatre, London on June 16, 1981. Bond had directed at Newcastle and the Royal Court, but the New Half Moon production was directed by Nick Hamm, although Bond attended some of the rehearsals. All three productions will be considered as providing substantial practical definitions of Bond's approach to theatre.

Bond's first play since *Saved* to be placed in a contemporary setting, *The Worlds* raised critical expectations. Comparisons between these two plays led many critics to view the more recent work as being concerned only with "moral abstractions, hence compromising Bond's ability to move us."[1] According to the critics instead of empathizing with the characters, Bond was seen to have created "comic-strip attitudes which would be funny if it was not for the awful conviction that we are intended to take them seriously."[2] However, there are dangers in juxtaposing *The Worlds* and *Saved*. Bond's later work resists comparison with his earlier naturalistic plays because of their different periods and styles. With *The Worlds*, Bond made his first attempt at assuming sole responsibility for putting an alternative approach of acting into operation in these "answer" plays.[3]

Bond's acting theories, of which the Public Soliloquy is a part, will be explored through an examination of the play's various productions.

The Worlds was written and produced at an important time in Britain's political history. The Labour Party, elected on February 28, 1974 with Harold Wilson as leader, was the first minority government since 1931. Hoping to increase his party's representation, Wilson held another General Election on October 10, 1974. Despite confident predictions of winning a larger majority, the Labour Party gained only eighteen more Members of Parliament than it held in the February election. Already suffering a blow to his confidence, Wilson tried to steer the government through these economically difficult times but, failing to do so, announced his resignation on March 16, 1976. His successor as prime minister was James Callaghan. Also politically floundering, Callaghan attempted to lead a Labour Party deeply divided on many key issues. This culminated in the 1978/9 "winter of discontent," a political nightmare which included a nationwide strike of truck drivers and regional stoppages of water and sewage workers, ambulance drivers and garbage collectors. This was the background against which *The Worlds* was written: a time of significant social upheaval in which radical discontent played a large part. These problems, along with Labour's inability to hold inflation down to single figures, led to the electorates' decision at the next general election on May 3, 1979. A confident, aggressive Margaret Thatcher became prime minister as head of a Conservative Party that had achieved the strongest election victory since the end of the Second World War. Bond's response to the "false optimism" created by the new government would be contained in his next play, *Restoration*.

The narrative of *The Worlds* is straight-forward. During a country weekend thrown for board members of the company TCC, its founder and managing director, John Trench, is kidnapped by terrorists. He is to be held hostage until the demands of striking workers at TCC are met. Trench's company directors take advantage of his absence to remove him from the board and offer the shares of the company on the stock exchange. Having escaped from his captors, Trench returns to TCC to find himself demoted and powerless to control his own company. Trench invites his colleagues to a dinner party at which he has promised to show them an oil painting of the directors. The portrait is unveiled to reveal a "seaside photographer's prop": a canvas with holes where heads ought to be, depicting a blonde girl and a muscle man set against a seaside background. After insulting them, Trench throws them out of his house. He then goes to live in the abandoned dwelling in which he had previously been imprisoned. An attempt is then made by the terrorists to capture TCC's chairman, planning to take their hostage to Trench's derelict home. By mistake they seize the chairman's chauffeur. During a rescue mission, the terrorists are captured and Trench shoots the kidnapped driver.

The Worlds has been likened by many critics to Shakespeare's *Timon of Athens*. Like Shakespeare's play, it focuses on an individual's conscious renunciation of organized, affluent society for a hermit's isolation. It is almost as if Bond had started with the premise about Trench, "What might have conceivably reduced a man to this condition."[4] *The Worlds* and *Timon of Athens* also share a narrative similarity. What H.J. Oliver has written in his introduction to Shakespeare's play might also be said of *The Worlds*:

> With an absolute minimum of chronological narrative, Shakespeare has set off against each other the reactions of one man to different situations, and the reactions of different men to the same situation.[5]

Similarly, Bond's play shows the change in Trench's response towards various aspects of his life following his kidnapping and reveals the assorted reactions of Kendal, Harris and Hubbard to the company take-over.

Bond also links his dramatic approach in this play with that of Molière:

> Molière worked always on a careful thesis, to an intelligent audience capable of using ideas, tempering their passions with wit and style, in order to—at least in some cases—turn bonfires in derelict places into lazer beams: Molière has an urgent, moral and political purpose. So he articulates and doesn't go in for romantic excesses in order to persuade you that he thinks: rather like someone who shouts because they believe this will make their logic clearer.[6]

Plays by Molière, such as *The Miser*, *The Misanthrope* and *Tartuffe*, contain scathing satirical attacks on hypocrisy, selfishness, self-importance and greed both in individuals and, more importantly, the society which helped form them. Like Molière, Bond explores contradictory impulses within the individual, for example with the businessmen. Bond has also compared *The Worlds*, through its use of Public Soliloquy, with Molière's stylistic artificiality.

Anna, one of the terrorists, states the play's central theme in *A Lecture*:

> Listen. There are two worlds. Most people think they live in one but they live in two. First there's the daily world in which we live. The world of appearance. There's law and order, right and wrong, good manners. How else could we live and work together? But there's also the *real* world. The world of power, machines, buying, selling, working. That world depends on capital: money! Money can do anything. It gives you the power of giants. The real world obeys the law of money. And there's a paradox about this law: whoever owns money is owned by it. A man buys a house. Does he own it? No, because to keep it he must get more money. And so the house owns him. The same is true of the clothes on your back and the food on your plate. Our lives, our minds, what we are, the way we see the world, are not shaped by human law but by the law of money.[7]

The play examines this concept of two "worlds" in terms of four groups of characters: John Trench himself; the directors, led by Hubbard, who instigate the take-over of TCC: the strikers, led by Terry; and the terrorists, led by Anna. Some critics maintain the play lacks authenticity "in human terms":

> The terrorists are most overtly utilitarian; the management figures are reminiscent of Keefe's cut-outs, and while Bond is clearly more at home with the strikers, they too have a uniformity of response which underlies their apparently differing individual reactions to the turn of events. Bond seems wary of allowing his characters to live, for fear that their social or political function will be compromised.[8]

Rejecting these criticisms, Bond maintains "some of the most vivid characters I've written are in *The Worlds*."[9] Before considering the solution through this play of the Public Soliloquy concept and reconstructing various productions directed by Bond or with his assistance, it is important to clarify the views of Trench, the directors, strikers and terrorists, keeping in mind this critical charge of inauthenticity. A study of these characters demonstrates that *The Worlds* reveals Bond's main concern as the realization of his political analysis within a human context.

Initially Trench represents the "slick, ruthless, gangster world of international business; a really vicious world."[10] His language reflects what Bond has referred to as "the mask under the face, not the mask on it."[11] Trench's rhetoric at the beginning of the play reveals his belief in a capitalist system. But after his kidnapping, Trench sees how he is manipulated by a capitalist structure and turns against the hypocrisy of his fellow board-members.

Part One, scene five, occurs in the boardroom. Hubbard, Kendal and Harris relate the administrative changes that have occurred whilst Trench has been away. Trench's response reveals the injustices that Bond confronts throughout the play, posing the question, "Who are the real terrorists?:"

> You make black white! Dirt clean! Evil Good! Pervert reason! My god terrorists stand things on their head. Turn values upside down. But the police go after them! You do it and vote yourself a rise! You don't rob a bank you have a cheque book! But no one hunts you, pillorizes you in the press.[12]

The directors play him at his own game, taking advantage of his absence to improve their own situation. Ethically, Trench has little redress, as their actions are simply a logical extension of his own capitalist principles.

Dramatically, the climax of Part One is the dinner party. Bond uses this grotesque incident to unmask the characters' true selves. It explores the businessman's selfish attitudes and, as with *Timon of Athens*, provides the host with an opportunity for revenge. All those involved in this horrific party belong to the property and business-owning class. It is in this scene that Bond demonstrates there is no honor, even amongst "colleagues," and so the party marks a significant development in Trench's understanding of his world.

Part Two sees Trench living, like Timon, as a recluse. Unlike Bond's Lear, Trench fails to transform this new understanding into a recognizable form from which others can learn. Indeed his isolation makes him bitter, withdrawn and fatalistic. As Margaret Biddle, in her study of Bond's work, indicates:

> [Even his] name suggests he is so "en-Trenched" in his class experience and his despair about human nature that he can only see one world, the one he has known.[13]

His language foreshadows the devastation of a nuclear war which was to dominate Bond's thoughts in *The War Plays*:

> The world's ended except for the crying. One day somebody in an office made a decision—probably minor—and history took a fatal turn. We were condemned. We didn't notice. The day passed and we went on. By the evening it was all over. The generation won't see the century out.[14]

Bond describes Trench as following a route leading "to a philosophy of despair, of seeing no meaning in life, of destruction":

> I'd like him to be played a bit like Samuel Beckett. He represents that sort of liberal culture . . . who were all the time being rude about the generals and the blimps who were in fact paying them and keeping their homes for them. Once the connection between the two gets broken then that culture becomes deeply reactionary because it is not a real culture. . .[15]

In these final moments of the play, Bond warns an audience of the dangers of responding aggressively without having planned a "*method* of change."[16] As Craig Dickson, the production assistant from the 1979 Newcastle production commented, it is especially important to observe the stage direction:[17]

> *The chauffeur is blinded by the light. Peers. Staggers. Sees picture. TRENCH's head is in the hole. Chauffeur tries to speak. No sound. TRENCH pushes his hand through the canvas. It holds a pistol. TRENCH shoots. The chauffeur is killed. TRENCH stares at him from the hole in the canvas. The pistol smokes.*[18]

It is appropriate that Trench kills the chauffeur *through* the photographer's seaside prop. Despite the change in his outward appearance (by peering through one of the picture's holes Trench is transformed to either a blonde girl or a muscle man) he still belongs to the upper class and is responsible for causing an innocent worker's death. In such a moment Bond mixes both tragic and comic elements, killing the chauffeur despite the picture's frivolous scene. Evoking complex responses is intentional on Bond's part:

> I wish in the play to trace back the responsibility for the chaos and danger of the present world to its real causes. These lie in the class that Trench represents—so Trench has to be the killer—and he kills by appearing out of the the painted clouds of his own ideological phantasies and cultural distortions: so the picture produces a real gun which kills.[19]

Characters who possess an overriding purpose in Bond's work do not necessarily lack individual qualities. Scene one of *The Worlds* exemplifies this when Kendal, Harris and Hubbard, who together firmly represent the world of the establishment, flatter JT in the hope of gaining further patronage. They employ various tactics which reveal their characteristics: Kendal praises JT, belittling his own contribution to the company's success; enthusiastic in the extreme, Harris endorses JT's every word; Hubbard, who is supportive of Trench, remains reserved throughout, very conscious of his own image.

The strikers, led by Terry, represent those seeking to improve wages by peaceful means through negotiation. Richard Rubenstein, an authority on conflict resolution, describes the nature of the discontent found amongst strikers:

> There are times when people interested in change—political change, social change—feel that not only is the state hostile but the masses are asleep. The question then becomes, how to wake up the masses? One answer is dramatic non-violent activity which galvanizes people.[20]

Such a statement is descriptive of the actions of Ray, John, Beryl and Terry who set an example to others through industrial action. Possibly the most significant scene that represents their position occurs in Part One, scene four. Here Terry discusses the situation and demonstrates, through "acted" scenarios, upper class control. As Philip Roberts argues, the group is carefully differentiated:

> Ray is for going back to work. He wants nothing to do with what he calls terrorism. Beryl tries to ease the situation by jokes and wavers with the argument. When formal discussion fails, John initially and Terry subsequently begin to offer Ray and Beryl parables designed to make

the issues clearer. . . The point is to show the logic of Terry's reasoning
and also to show that the first problem is one of persuading the
oppressed that is their condition.[21]

Ultimately, these parables, Terry's representation of a policeman, his use of Beryl's purse and a few of his pound notes, are
aimed at educating an audience. For despite different levels of
understanding, the workers are on strike actively standing for
what they believe. Bond clarifies the situation in a letter:

> Its important that this [scene with the money] isnt patronizing to the
> people to whom Terry is speaking: he tells them what they already
> know, they're not like eskimos looking at their first television set and
> wondering how the little people got inside: it should be more as if
> they're being given an illustration about, say, electricity: they wish to
> appear confident and able to wire a plug, but they're careful to learn
> which wire is live, which is the earthed wire and so on. . .[22]

The "Negotiation Speech" of workers and management is
juxtaposed with John attempting to sell Terry his over-priced,
defective motorbike. This ironical incident captures one of the
play's central themes—capitalism imposes an irrational instinct
on man, where bargaining over wages and the life of an innocent man can be discussed in the same context as the sale of a
bike.

The strike's futility is seen during the final moments of *The
Worlds*, when Terry, John and Beryl sit together on a bench.
They have accomplished their demands, but as a result of sup-
porting actions that have caused the chauffeur's death. In
"Press Release," his final speech, Terry reveals an understand-
ing of the problem with society:

> The poor are starving. The rich are getting ready to blow it up. Terror-
> ists threaten with guns? We do it with bombs. One well-heeled Ameri-
> can with his finger on the button. That's sick. And there's worse than
> that. The ignorance we live in. We don't understand what we are or
> what we do. That's more dangerous than bombs.[23]

While it might be argued that this represents the subjugation of
character to Bond's political rhetoric, Terry's speech can be
seen as the outburst of a radical who has wanted to redress
what he sees as social inequities and been denied the
opportunity.

Richard Rubenstein has provided this definition of those attracted to terrorism:

> We would like to think of them [terrorists] as monsters. But when we look and see who they are they are generally youngish people, ranging in age between 15 and 35. In many ways they are not unlike us. . .[24]

Certainly there is nothing extraordinary about Anna, Lisa and Michael, who represent this violent alternative. Unhappy with the situation at TCC, they rebel by seizing hostages, forcing management to listen to the strikers' demands. Their direct aggression is, significantly, reflective of Trench's capitalist assault on his workforce, "When you come down to it Trench relies on force as much as any terrorist."[25] In production, Bond maintains, the apparent didacticism of Anna's long speeches (Part One, scene four—the reading of the ultimatum, and Part Two, scene five—the lecture)—disappears:

> The first long didactic speech is drowned out by a machine, and by distorted incomprehension. The second long didactic speech is said twice—but it is said in a madhouse.[26]

Bond also suggests how the speeches should operate in performance:

> [The speeches are] the two ends of the key: the toothed end which turns the lock is the content of the speech—the end which is clasped in the hand is the situation: and the toothed end comes to life (in the play) because it is held in the hand—the situation: this is what gives it its viability. And so it should be very simple—and easy on the ear.[27]

Jenny S. Spencer observes that the terrorists in *The Worlds*, like Hecuba in *The Woman*, are able to understand their class position "in a way that allows them to act and to escape . . . being the victims of history and not circumstance":

> These characters are not automatically endowed with an enlightened perspective, but come to it through the learning process offered by the concrete experiences and social relationships of the play. It is a practical knowledge, never a purely conceptual one, which issues in and provides a model for action.[28]

In this play terrorist activity ultimately fails because Trench, Anna, Michael and Lisa have not confronted the source of their political problems, an inequitable society based on class divisions. The chauffeur's murder is representative of this failure to understand their situation. Although Trench carries out the killing, the chauffeur's presence has been made possible by the terrorists who have highjacked the worker by mistake. As with the strikers, who attempt social reform, the terrorists do not tackle the cause of their suffering, the structure of the society against which they are fighting. Their aim is simply to resolve society's difficulties without confronting the origin of the problem, the way society is organized.

The most significant acting theory Bond developed for *The Worlds* was the Public Soliloquy (PS.) This notion was explored later in the songs for *Restoration*. In *The Activist Papers*, Bond describes the purpose of this technique:

> In *The Worlds* I tried to find contemporary equivalents for Shakespeare's soliloquy. I wanted to provide a means of informed, personal comment on the play. At the same time I wanted to show the force of history, the cause of historical change.[29]

The PS in *The Worlds* can be expressed only by individuals whose insight penetrates beyond appearance and into the actual workings of society. Consequently, it is only used by the strikers, terrorists and Trench, who, ultimately, learns about how society operates. The PS occurs most notably in Part Two, scenes three and four. "A Public Soliloquy," "A Workman's Biography" and "A Speech" all demonstrate Terry's responsibility to both the situation around him and his class position. For Bond, the origin of the PS came with the play's artificiality:

> *The Worlds* is such an artificial play that someone having a Public Soliloquy is like someone having an aria. There are no songs in the play, no tunes and so the PS contains functions that they might have performed.[30]

Bond offers this advice to an actor who has the task of alternating between both his role and social comment:

> I think to make Public Soliloquy work, we also have to create new conventions. . . If the audience see a disparity between you as the future-character and the character you are actually playing—perhaps they'll feel sad or burdened at the thought of the effort it would take to bridge the two, the difficulty of social change. But perhaps you should play the

Public Soliloquy more lightly than the rest of the part—play it with great
simplicity and naturalness—"of course things will be otherwise"—almost
as if you were reminiscing, remembering contentedly, the future?—but
with an edge of tension that denotes that movement will be necessary.[31]

Part One, scene four in which Terry, Beryl, Ray and John
discuss their actions, have been described by Bond as a "group
public soliloquy."

Whole characters or groups could be permeated with public soliloquy
so that we feel they're both in and outside their time and aren't eternal
prisoners of the present appearance of things.[32]

This technique requires a different style of acting but Bond
does not see the difficulty of playing the PS:

The mask of the Greek theatre is an artifice, so is the blank verse of
Jacobean theatre. They work because they are necessary to tell the truth
(in those theatres.). . . In theatre we have to create new conventions if
we want to wear masks and speak blank verse. So I think to make PS
work we also have to create new conventions.[33]

Although this alternative style of presentation was not fully
developed, Bond recognized the need for the PS to be acted
differently. Louise Kerr, an actor from the Newcastle production of *The Worlds*, observes:

Public Soliloquies were to do with being unemotive and clear but connected, not being impassioned or emoting . . . that the message is clear
and you stand back and look at what you are saying.[34]

As an attempt has been made to define the Public Soliloquy,
it would be convenient if I could describe an acting style for
The Worlds. However, no such water-tight theory existed at this
point in Bond's work as a director. What can be explored are
the various characteristic and stylistic patterns of acting that
emerged at Newcastle and in London. By examining these productions alongside each other, it will be possible to explore
whether Bond constructed a consistent model which he developed during rehearsals and subsequent productions of the play.

Prior to *The Worlds*, Bond conducted a series of improvisation sessions at Newcastle University. These culminated in a
short play about the city of Belfast. Ken Price, who participated

in these workshops and played Kendal in the subsequent production of *The Worlds*, commented that, even at this point,
Bond talked about developing an acting style:

> Bond had an idea in his head, something about Belfast. We evolved it,
> with him guiding and shaping the storyline, adding the poetry to give a
> symmetry and symbolism using us as "types." It became a finished piece
> and had one performance which lasted for about twenty minutes. . .
> There was no judgement made about the quality of the acting. He was
> just interested in working for a certain kind of honesty.[35]

A number of improvisations were explored in preparation for
the piece on Belfast. These workshops do not relate directly to
The Worlds but contribute to an overall sense of what Bond was
working for at that time. Price recalls some of the most significant exercises:

> All sorts of people came to it from all sorts of life in the University.
> One improvisation involved striking a match and as you held it you had
> to tell a story of your life. Some people came up with something and
> dared to let the match burn down. Others would be frozen by the
> idea. . . Another was a mime. A man was going into a shop to buy a suit
> for his wedding. The situation was that the trousers would fit but the
> jacket would be too small.[36]

Another exercise involved each character in the scenario carrying a chair as they entered the space. According to Price, this
was "crucial to an understanding of the burden they carried."
Debbie Bestwick, a participant in these workshops who also
played Ms Linnell in *The Worlds* at Newcastle, recalls the process as a stimulating one:

> Bond spent a lot of time working on images, something I found
> extremely useful. We spent the first few days doing exercises on
> imagery for the stage. We sat around in a circle discussing stories from
> newspaper clippings. We discussed gesture and then spent a lot of time
> getting these images right. This was conducted over a week full-time
> and, called *The Pool of Blood*, it was given a performance.[37]

These workshops are significant in showing Bond's preoccupa-
tion with condensation, summing up the essence of people's
lives and conveying this understanding in simple and direct
terms. He was also concerned, as can be seen from the suit and
chair exercises, in working out how to convey these impressions

through dramatic metaphors. The improvisations, as Price recalls, were also designed to "provoke a response by confronting people with themselves."

According to Louise Kerr, who played Anna in the Newcastle production, the play was given a fairly intensive six-week rehearsal period. This culminated in the first production of *The Worlds* at the Newcastle Playhouse, opening March 8, 1979 presented by the University's Theatre Society. The NUTS was comprised of students from both the University and Polytechnic:

> Part of his brief [as writer in residence] was to write and direct a play with the students. This was made known to us all and we auditioned. The University had a theatre society and the Polytechnic its own drama course.[38]

Many students were attracted to his work through Bond's notoriety in the University. One of the ex-students has commented:

> I remember thinking when I first arrived, the professors in the English department were guardians of the sacred flame of literature. Then this man came in who said things like, "Beckett's philosophy is questionable," and to a distinguished Shakespeare Fellow, "You don't know what you are talking about, of course Shakespeare had political ideas." A strong tension developed between Bond and the University.[39]

The Worlds was written for performance by young people and both the Newcastle and Royal Court productions were acted by students. According to Bond, students are in "an extreme learning condition and so we have to teach young people to change society."[40] Critics of Bond's work might argue that in directing his play Bond was attempting to manipulate students and control their creative instincts. However, there is no evidence of such coercion. On the contrary it could be suggested that Bond's intentions were artistic. For example, it is worth considering the theatrical effect of young persons playing older characters such as Trench. Graham Blockey, who played Trench, states that no effort was made at more mature characterization: "There was no attempt to age Trench, even though at the age of twenty-two I was playing a fifty-five year old businessman."[41] Theoretically this disparity between actor and character is useful to Bond's form of theatre. But in practice, as

Price has commented, the casting of young actors may have resulted in a lack of experience and skill in the production: "I am not sure how many of us as students were equipped to come to terms with the style of acting Bond was suggesting."[42] Another factor in Bond's decision to use young actors was his conscious desire to escape the approach professional actors often took with his plays. Craig Dickson stated:

> Edward's view of us was that, as students, we had not been contaminated by a drama school training or working in the professional theatre. He believed that the truth of his writing would become very apparent to us, and because of the actor's naturalness, the overwhelming forces of the argument would shine through the performances in the words.[43]

Far from being manipulative, Bond's use of student actors allowed him to gain a "fresh approach" to his work in performance something which could not be provided by actors with extensive training and professional exposure.[44]

Rehearsals at Newcastle were textually-based with little external experimental work. One of the actors described the process:

> Rehearsals contained different interpretations of the same piece of text; what could they be saying, what could be behind this, what are they saying about themselves and each other. The text was very closely looked at. Any particular line had six meanings.[45]

However, Bond did some improvisations designed to explore qualities of a character. These exercises always sprung from the text:

> One of his exercises was to do with showing the character's need and desire. For example, you had a pound note on the floor and you cannot get to it but you need that money. So the exercise was to do with self-expression based on a socio-economic need.[46]

Bond employed several techniques aimed at shifting an actor's interpretations of the character. Kerr relates an approach Bond used to help with Anna's speech about "appearance" and "reality" in Part Two, scene five:

> The arguments were difficult so it had to be simple but also honest. To put this across, Edward would sit and pretend to be a child at my feet and I would have to deliver it so a child would understand it.[47]

Price recalls body language as being an especially important characteristic of Bond's acting style:

> ... The moment Pru strips is very important to him [Kendal] physically. Bond had Kendal lying on the stage drinking, not attempting to stop it or react in any way. These were visual keys for the audience, little shock tactics.[48]

Quite early in the rehearsal process, Bond "blocked" much of the play. Staging became a significant factor in his handling of the production:

> I made ... formal patterns with the actors at Newcastle. I grouped them on the stage to give structures, but only at certain times. Then when the "madness" erupted from time to time, I let the formality collapse into chaos (though actually it was highly engineered and controlled.)[49]

Kerr maintains that the workers had a "poetic quality" lacked by the businessmen:

> There was a differentiation between the businessmen and the terrorists. This was mainly through the symbolic use of space; the businessmen owned the territory. They were played quite stiffly, rather caricatured. They were quite mannequin-like in a way.[50]

Like its production at Newcastle, *The Worlds* at the Royal Court Theatre Upstairs was staged by young people without any attempt at creating mature characterization. According to Geoff Church, who played Trench at the Royal Court, "he did not want to age the acting at all. On one level he wanted people to see it was me."[51] Auditions for the Activists consisted of a number of exercises:

> We had to impersonate one of our parents in front of the whole group, to come up with a sort of psychological gesture and a noise. Then he got us all to impersonate him.[52]

Bond emphasized that the most important element in rehearsals was that actors as individuals should have a response to both the script and the world at large. This is a central issue in Bond's form of theatre. Although this social and political awareness was stressed at Newcastle, Bond's emphasis on it at

the Royal Court made it an important distinction in the production. One of the actors recalled such an occasion:

> I remember an afternoon discussing politics in general and the politics
> of the play. In the conversation I said, "I don't know I can see it from
> both sides." Bond said, "That is not good enough. You have got to
> have an attitude if you are alive in this world. The whole of politics is
> the way we organise ourselves."[53]

This idea, of having politically motivated actors, connects with
Bond's notion of character as expressed in *The Activists Papers*.
By forcing actors to be politically aware, Bond stressed the
necessity of showing a life defined by its social and economic
realities. According to Peter Hall's diaries, the creation of a
political atmosphere in auditions for *The Woman* was clear from
the outset.[54] It may be no coincidence that younger or amateur
actors are more responsive to Bond's work. From seeing many
of his plays in performance, it has been my experience that
many students, without the demands of professional theatre,
have made themselves more accessible to many of Bond's performance techniques. This was the case with the two initial productions of *The Worlds* where instead of using rehearsal time to
explore characterization, Bond worked on the social context.
Geoff Church recalls:

> ... Bart Peel, as Lord Bigdyke, said to Edward he could not find his
> character. Edward replied, "How much time as a person do you spend
> wandering around thinking "Who am I?." Do what the character does
> in the play and in rehearsal try that out."[55]

Bond also placed a great emphasis on textual precision. But
was this useful to the actor? Diana Judd, playing Pru, believed it
was, leaving "not one question mark":

> We spent most of the time in rehearsal analyzing each line to its maxi-
> mum. This is very good for the actor because you knew exactly what
> you were saying, why you were saying it.[56]

Likewise, Dan Hildebrand, Terry at the Royal Court, remembers: "Bond would sit down, go through a speech with me and
say, 'This is where the thought changes and there is a different
idea here.'"[57] Church stated that Bond went back to teaching
the basic problems of acting including relaxation and posture—

something not covered in rehearsals at Newcastle. Bond's interest in developing actor-training was the relationship of his text to acting-style:

> To solve an actor's problems of speech in relation to a particular text is very interesting for a writer because it teaches him more about his own text.[58]

The possibility of discovering new insights into his own work and how the actor manages the text is one of the attractions for Bond both as writer and director.

As with the production at Newcastle, Bond did some experimental work which served the script's needs. Church recalls working in this way on one of Trench's speeches at the end of the play:

> I remember having real problems with this speech and so Edward got me to scrabble around on the floor as if I were trying to tear the floor up whilst I was trying to find what I was looking for in the speech.[59]

Belinda Blanchard, playing Beryl, states that improvised situations were established occasionally to explore textual ideas. The relevance of one such improvisation is immediately apparent:

> Bond got us into groups of three: the terrorists, people on a plane and negotiators. We were on a plane and I was pregnant. The point of the improvisation was that we had to work out how to get around the situation and how much of what the highjackers were telling us was true.[60]

A significant amount of rehearsal time was spent on Trench's dinner party. This scene caused difficulty which, according to Church, Bond resolved as the solution lay outside their experience as actors:

> Edward came up with this radical solution three days before we opened, that once the picture was exposed, everyone in the scene should revert to being three years old. For example, Hubbard ended up on the floor rocking and sucking his thumb.[61]

Church stated that the scene became "unnaturalistic," concerned with the emergence of "people's bizarre characteristics."[62] Such a technique can be interpreted as a descent into madness, caused by profound shock. As a result of the experi-

ment, these new reactions from the businessmen were retained
in performance. The actors continued with Bond's notion that,
confronted by the truth, characters such as the businessmen
experience profound psychological degeneration seeking
escape from political realities through unusual actions. This
scene contains an inversion of the anticipated result of an incident. It is a technique which is a familiar motif in Bond's work
having overtones of Hatch's actions in *The Sea* or Mrs Lewis's
laughter on seeing Brian Tebham's corpse in *Jackets II*.

The professional premiere of *The Worlds* at the New Half
Moon Theatre, London was directed by Nick Hamm with Bond
providing directorial advice on a number of occasions. According to Daniel Baron Cohen—Hamm's assistant on the production who subsequently directed *The Worlds* at Manchester University using a woman to play Trench—Bond made only a few
visits because at that time he was directing *Restoration* at the
Royal Court:

> I can only recall Edward being at about three or four rehearsals and I
> seem to remember him asking the kind of questions that challenged all
> that had been done.[63]

Unlike the other productions, it used a company of nine adult
actors who doubled and sometimes tripled the roles. Ian McDiarmid played both Trench and Terry, a coupling of roles which
emphasized the characters' different approaches to the play's
situation. Whereas Trench does not violate the capitalist system
by breaking its rules, Terry constantly engages in class struggle
although he is convinced by the end of the play that it is a general complacency which ensures the retention of our current
social structure. Barrie Houghton played Hubbard/Ray, Robin
Hooper played Kendall, Harris/John was played by Robin
Soans, the three roles of Ms Linnell/Sylvia/Anna by Johanna
Kirby, Rory Edwards played Michael/Gate, Sian Thomas
appeared as Lisa/Pru/Beryl, Marian/Lady Armstrong was
Linda Spurrier and Steven Crossley played the Police
Chief/The Perfect Waiter and the White Figure. The stage
manager, Heather Peace, played Barway.

The Worlds went into rehearsal in May with the majority of
time spent in textual analysis. McDiarmid commented on the
acting style that emerged:

> We try to get rid of naturalistic detail. It doesn't mean its like clock-
> work. It has to be felt through and acted through. But he [Bond]
> doesn't want anything to be dissipated in naturalistic detail.[64]

McDiarmid emphasized that this anti-naturalistic style did not
mean the play's characters were unreal:

> There's nothing inhuman about Trench. It's the situation of a human
> being you're watching. He may speak in platitudes, but that's because
> that's the way these people talk.[65]

Robin Hooper also commented on this alternative approach to
acting:

> [Bond] wanted us to say the lines clearly, audibly and to be still. Bond's
> style is very clear with a precise way of speaking. It is very, very spe-
> cific. . . Bond gets very anxious and rather threatened by actors who do
> too much with his material. . . All you have to bring is your
> intelligence, confidence and something of your emotional truth.[66]

The design for *The Worlds* at Newcastle, by Hayden Griffin,
who had previously designed *The Woman*, concentrated on simplicity in stage design, literally stripping back to the theatre's
walls. Ken Price describes the staging of the Newcastle production:

> The Newcastle Playhouse has a very big open stage with an open audi-
> torium. When stripped down to the bare minimum, which it was for
> *The Worlds*, it has a brick wall that continues all the way round to the
> foyer. Bond exposed that and they built trompe l'oeil walls to the side
> which joined the back wall of the theatre to the sides of the audito-
> rium. There was a clock on the back wall which was about six feet in
> diameter.[67]

According to Craig Dickson, the clock was set at ten minutes to
ten, the time the production ended, "as though it had been
happening in real time. Once the show finished, you had to go
out and act."[68] Apart from chairs, the setting was dominated by
a long boardroom table, "about twenty or thirty foot in length"
the top of which was covered in walnut.[69] This was the only

item remaining on stage constantly. Otherwise, the area was bare: "A late addition towards the end of the rehearsal period was a circus floor, a white tarpaulin square with ropes."[70] This helped the terrorists define their space, about six foot by four foot, which was "set up with rucksacks, sleeping bags and a chair."[71] Their area was also lit by a gobo helping them keep within these spatial restrictions.

As with the set, lighting at Newcastle was simple. A bright white light was used throughout the play:

> The lighting was done using a square rig rather than the University's rig. [The lanterns] were not hidden from view. Instead they hung on scaffolding bars just below the gantry. I have never seen the stage lit so well. It was crystal clear. Very stark.[72]

Consistent with Bond's philosophy as seen in the production of *The Woman*, it is worth noting the intervals between scenes were lit. This suggests that Bond did not want the theatrical experience to be illusory in any way. Price recalls the lighting was "not very atmospheric," and that at one point "the light was shone on the audience."[73]

The Royal Court Theatre Upstairs is a very small theatre with seating banked up on either side. The setting, designed by Eamon D'arcy, is described by one of the actors:

> It was simply painted white. The windows were exposed. The lighting too was completely white. The whole set was very stark. The only dominant thing, apart from a few chairs, was the picture Trench unveils.[74]

In a letter, Bond has described the Theatre Upstairs as a "room."[75] By this he means a small space in which the play's events are magnified so the division between theatrical illusion and reality are broken down. This occurred in the penultimate scene where Bond used a device, similar to the effect of the clock at Newcastle, to confront an audience with the play's relevance:

> The lights and sounds of the helicopters and guns were outside on the roof. The room had real windows which opened out onto the roofs of the neighbouring buildings. . . Towards the end one of the terrorists ran in, dashed across the floor and smashed one of the windows with a rifle butt—and the scene opened out onto the roofs of the Sloane quar-

ter and the noises of the city and of the attack came in. The last scene was played with the smashed open window into the city and the actors sitting among the broken glass. This isnt sensationalism—but analytic of the audience's situation: that the problems of the play were to them as real as the city.[76]

The first time it was used, this effect had repercussion with the theatre's neighbours:

A crowd of them came to the stage door and were very angry. I remember them shouting and threatening. But I wasnt pursuing sensationalism: it was just the consequence of the Theatre Event approach.[77]

Nick Hamm's setting at the New Half Moon, was also white with simply a boardroom table and a few chairs.

The Worlds creates a range of complex ideas, but, for Bond as director, the necessary acting style should demonstrate these ideas as simply as possible. This does not suggest that a simplified approach to acting reduces Bond's insights to a trivial level. Simplicity is just a further practical element of his concept of a "Rational Theatre;" a theatre which shows the *cause* of a character's response to a given situation. For example, Bond suggests that the acting of Trench's unveiling of the picture is a scene dependent on its structure. Necessarily this affects the acting style of the production:

You must take it apart in rehearsal to find out the interlocking nature, the structure of its bits and pieces: then they can come together to produce their own energy. If this isnt done, the actors will apply energy from outside, they will "agitate things," produce hectic, comic business—but really the fever isnt interested in making jokes, it just burns with its own thoroughness: so the scene must be fast and funny, and *absolutely resting on its structure*. Otherwise there is that most dismal spectacle of all in the theatre: the Grand Prix motor-racing driver gets out of his beautiful machine and pushes it to make it go faster: we know that, for all his frantic efforts, the trouble is he doesnt understand his machine.[78]

Bond suggests a technique for Part One, scene four where Terry explains to the other workers how the essential composition of society is based on theft. His concern is that this scene does not become patronizing: "its a description of the people's lives":

Perhaps you should try (in rehearsals) various ways of handling the money: very angrily, then very gently—to suggest the human relations that are impregnated in the money.[79]

The exercise suggests how "objective and subjective can be written down together and the interaction between them demonstrated."[80] This principle is fundamental to an understanding of Bond's practical work in the theatre. By demonstrating both the situation and a character's response to it, the political and social dynamic can be revealed.

Central to the play's overall design is an "aesthetic device chosen for its toy-like simplicity."[81] Bond has described this as a circus drum-roll:

One of the structural devices is the idea of the circus, music-hall or execution-platform drum-roll. It takes the form of motor bikes, helicopters and the verbal build-ups to the unveiling etc—and its contrasted with silence and very "articulate" passages.[82]

Such an approach can be used in a number of places throughout the play concluding with the picture and the chauffeur's death. According to Bond, the drum-roll commences in the "message-reading" scene (Part One, scene three)—beginning miles and miles away behind the hills and slowly crescendoing until it drowns out the voices."[83]

Finally, Bond discusses the importance of TEs in *The Worlds*:

Consider the relationship between the chairs in the play. Or the tea which is so elaborately served in the board room and the bottles of "pop" served in scenes 2/4. Why is the rose given water to drink in a silver vase . . . and how is the vase set down on the table? Audiences are not consciously putting these moments together as they watch the play: but they increase the audience awareness as they go through the play—and are then left to work with the audience after the play.[84]

Even at this stage in Bond's development as a writer and director, his concern is with addressing an audience through metaphors. The connection between physical properties within the play can produce TEs but Bond is concerned that this term does not become meaningless:

I think there is a danger of playing patterns. TEs are there [in the plays] and it is very helpful to know they are there. But they are not like frameworks and the plays fitted into them. . . Sometimes I hear in rehearsals, "That's like that moment when. . ." That's fine if that is helpful. . . But if the point is to play the comparison or repetition then I think it might be unhelpful.[85]

So what is the connection, if any, between the PS and the TE?:

I had the idea of the PS before I had the idea of TE. The PS was necessary to put into the play an interpretation which cannot be read into the content of the play. The TE is much more theatrically competent than the PS, the TE is here and now, but it did have its origins there.[86]

Despite varied criticism, *The Worlds* is important in Bond's development as both playwright and director. My impression is that Bond seems to be exploring a consistent strategy in his treatment of actors. Both in Newcastle and London, he had the opportunity of working with young people who were unaffected by the constraints of professional theatre. Yet, at the same time, Bond worked with skilled designers bringing higher standards to "amateur" theatre and continuing to formulate his acting theories, experimenting in ways that would have been impossible in the professional theatre. It may be that his combination of student actors in an environment committed to learning is the ideal setting for Bond's plays.

Although Bond was comparatively free of restrictions during *The Worlds*, problems were to hamper him creatively in his next professional production at the Royal Court—*Restoration*.

Notes

1 Michael Billington, *Guardian* 17 June 1981: 10.

2 Christopher Hudson, *New Standard* 18 June 1981: 26.

3 Initially Bond separated his work into three groups. "Problem plays" begin with *The Pope's Wedding* and end with *The Sea*. *Bingo, The Fool* and *The Woman* form the middle group which deal with the problems of culture. From the time of *The Worlds* Bond has written "answer plays" of which he has said: "I have stated the problems as clearly as I can—now let's try and look at what answers are applicable." Edward Bond quoted in Malcolm Hay and Philip Roberts, *Bond: A Study of his Plays* (London: Methuen, 1980) 266.

4 H. J. Oliver (ed.) in *Timon of Athens* by William Shakespeare (London: Methuen, 1979) xlvii.

5 Oliver xlviii.

6 Edward Bond, letter to Erika Beck, 19 December 1986.

7 Edward Bond, *The Worlds with The Activists Papers* (London: Methuen, 1980) 76/7.

8 M. Martin, "The Search for a Form; Recently Published Plays," *Critical Quarterly* 23 (4) 1981: 56.

9 Edward Bond, letter to author, 22 April 1990.

10 Edward Bond, interview with David L. Hirst, quoted in *Edward Bond* by David L. Hirst (London: Macmillan, 1985) 153.

11 Edward Bond quoted in Hirst 153.

12 Bond *The Worlds* 39.

13 Margaret Biddle, "Learning and Teaching for Change: The Plays of Edward Bond," diss. University of York, 1985, 219/220.

14 Bond *The Worlds* 75/6.

15 Edward Bond, interview with David L. Hirst, quoted in Hirst 152/3.

16 Edward Bond, "Author's Preface to 'Lear'" *Bond Plays: Two* (London: Methuen, 1978) 11.

17 *The Worlds* 82 quoted by Craig Dickson, personal interview, 25 April 1990.

18 Bond *The Worlds* 82.

19 Edward Bond, letter to Hilde Klein Hagen, 12 September 1987.

20 Professor Richard Rubenstein, *Against the State* BBC Radio 4, Wednesday May 2, 1990.

21 Philip Roberts, "The Search for Epic Drama: Edward Bond's Recent Work," *Modern Drama* 24 (4) 1981: 463.

22 Edward Bond, letter to Erika Beck, 19 December 1986.

23 Bond *The Worlds* 84.

24 Professor Richard Rubenstein, *Against the State* BBC Radio 4 Wednesday May 2, 1990.

25 Bond *The Worlds* 33.

26 Edward Bond, letter to Georges Bas, 3 October 1989.

27 Edward Bond, letter to Georges Bas, 3 October 1989.

28 Jenny S. Spencer, "Edward Bond's Dramatic Strategies," *Contemporary English Drama* 19 1981: 131.

29 Bond, *The Worlds with The Activists Papers* 137.

30 Edward Bond, personal interview, 12 June 1990.

31 Edward Bond, letter to author, 22 April 1990.

32 Bond *Activists* 141.

33 Edward Bond, letter to author, 22 April 1990.

34 Louise Kerr, personal interview, 20 April 1990.

35 Ken Price, personal interview, 20 April 1990.

36 Ken Price, personal interview, 20 April 1990.

37 Debbie Bestwick, personal interview, 26 June 1990.

38 Louise Kerr, personal interview, 20 April 1990.

39 Craig Dickson, personal interview, 25 April 1990.

40 Edward Bond quoted in the *Eltham Times* 29 November 1979: (S) 3.

41 Graham Blockey, personal interview, 14 May 1990.

42 Ken Price, personal interview, 20 April 1990.

43 Craig Dickson, personal interview, 25 April 1990.

44 Louise Kerr, personal interview, 20 April 1990.

45 Louise Kerr, personal interview, 20 April 1990.

46 Louise Kerr, personal interview, 20 April 1990.

47 Louise Kerr, personal interview, 20 April 1990.

48 Ken Price, personal interview, 20 April 1990.

49 Edward Bond, letter to author, 22 April 1990.

50 Louise Kerr, personal interview, 20 April 1990.

51 Geoff Church, personal interview, 8 May 1990.

52 Geoff Church, personal interview, 8 May 1990.

53 Geoff Church, personal interview, 8 May 1990.

54 [Bond] actually asks each of the actors auditioning for his new play what their politics are." *Peter Hall's Diaries–The Story of a Dramatic Battle* ed. John Goodwin, (Hamish Hamilton, 1984) 342.

55 Geoff Church, personal interview, 13 April 1990.

56 Diana Judd, personal interview, 13 April 1990.

57 Dan Hildebrand, personal interview, 2 May 1990.

58 Edward Bond quoted in *Auckland Star*, 30 January 1980.

59 Geoff Church, personal interview, 8 May 1990.

60 Belinda Blanchard, personal interview, 24 April 1990.

61 Geoff Church, personal interview, 8 May 1990.

62 Geoff Church, personal interview, 8 May 1990.

63 Daniel Baron Cohen, personal interview, 19 June 1990.

64 Ian McDiarmid quoted in "Rehearsing Optimism," by Jane Bryce *Leveller*, (60) July 1981: 18/19.

65 Ian McDiarmid quoted in *Leveller*.

66 Robin Hooper, personal interview, 1 May 1990.

67 Ken Price, personal interview, 20 April 1990.

68 Craig Dickson, personal interview, 25 April 1990.

69 Craig Dickson, personal interview, 25 April 1990.

70 Ken Price, personal interview, 20 April 1990.

71 Louise Kerr, personal interview, 20 April 1990.

72 Craig Dickson, personal interview, 25 April 1990.

73 Ken Price, personal interview, 20 April 1990.

74 Geoff Church, personal interview, 8 May 1990.

75 Edward Bond, letter to author, 22 April 1990.

76 Edward Bond, letter to author, 22 April 1990.

77 Edward Bond, letter to author, 22 April 1990.

78 Edward Bond, letter to Erika Beck, 19 December 1986.

79 Edward Bond, letter to Erika Beck, 19 December 1986.

80 Edward Bond, letter to Erika Beck, 19 December 1986.

81 Edward Bond, letter to Erika Beck, 19 December 1986.

82 Edward Bond, letter to Georges Bas, 25 February 1989.

83 Edward Bond, letter to Erika Beck, 19 December 1986.

84 Edward Bond, letter to Erika Beck, 12 December 1986.

85 Edward Bond, personal interview, 12 June 1990.

86 Edward Bond, personal interview, 12 June 1990.

Chapter Three

Restoration

There are a number of significant differences between *The Worlds* and *Restoration*, both in style and setting. For example, *The Worlds* is rooted firmly in "modern times" whereas *Restoration* occurs more loosely in "England, eighteenth century—or another place at another time."[1] *Restoration*, in its first production at the Royal Court Theatre, London, on July 21, 1981 was billed as a "musical," a "festive comedy" and, in the printed text, a "pastoral," very far removed from the industrial disputations of *The Worlds*. However, Bond suggests similarities do exist between the plays' apparently different landscapes. One connection is through the plays' language:

> I would have said that the language Lord Are and his associates use in some way relates to the language the businessmen use at the beginning of *The Worlds*. Although that is a completely different world, in a curious way they are using language similarly.[2]

A thematic parallel between *Restoration* and Bond's previous work was made by a critic who commented after seeing the 1981 production:

> Bond is a dark, demanding dramatist whose plays concentrate on violence and human exploitation and although this new one is set in the eighteenth century and in the style of Restoration comedy, Bond has not abandoned his familiar themes.[3]

Both *The Worlds* and *Restoration* are consistent in showing society's prevailing capitalist structure which, in Bond's opinion, lacks an understanding of itself and benefits only a minority.

The play received a mixed reception from both critics and public. For many, the 1981 production was only redeemed by the acting of the main characters and the singing of Debbie

Bishop as Rose. But others thought differently, such as Michael
Billington in the *Guardian*, who commented: "*Restoration* towers
like a colossus," and "it is a very long time since I have come
out of the Royal Court feeling that I have seen something not
merely promising but rich in achievement."[4] The production
also represented a significant turning point for Bond as director; it was the first he had undertaken using song. By so doing,
he used rock music of the twentieth century to comment upon
the eighteenth century world of the play. The relevance of this
production choice to the acting style and the play's method will
be explored along with a consideration of the physical elements
of the production. Attention will also be given to the 1988/9
production performed by the Royal Shakespeare Company,
directed by Roger Michell but with additional direction by Bond
prior to its transfer from Stratford-upon-Avon to London.
Among the important qualities of this second production were
the additions and deletions Bond made to the text. In many
cases these changes give an altered perception of characters
such as the Parson and Mrs Hedges.

This play was Bond's response to the British General Election
of 1979 in which the Conservatives won a resounding victory.
But why does Bond find it necessary to plunder the distant
world of "period" comedy to write a scathing attack on our present society? *Restoration* attempts to use the veneer of eighteenth century England not to escape the tensions that Bond
believes still exist in our modern world, but rather to expose
them. For example, the Ares, Mr Hardache, his daughter and
the Parson represent the individuals in control of society;
Frank, Bob, Rose, Mrs Hedges and a number of minor characters are those caught up in their power. This play tackles the
timeless issues of upper class domination over the working class
and so we find Bond's political dialectic as relevant to eighteenth century surroundings as a contemporary setting. Bond
has commented on the rationale behind the writing of the play:

> I wanted to write a play set in Restoration themes. These are still
> received almost totally uncritically in the theatre. The opportunism of
> the characters is applauded. Humour is taken as a self-consciousness
> which disarms the wicked and also in a way justifies them in their
> exploration of others. So their "silliness" makes them both socially

harmless and entitles them to their positions as exploiters. Tragedy is obviously excluded. Compare the simpleton in *Beaux Stratagem* with Lear's fool.[5]

Despite the claim of one critic, who believes that "any resemblance to Restoration types is really only superficial," parallels do exist between Bond's play and the characters and techniques of late seventeenth century English drama.[6] But despite its title, it needs to be emphasized that *Restoration* is set in the *eighteenth* century and therefore also contains a mixture of period dramatic styles. Lord Are, for example, is a classic figure from the plays of Wycherley and Etherege, whereas Hardache is representative of the upwardly mobile, speculative classes of the eighteenth century. Bond's purpose in forcing these two historically different figures together is to show the repressive hold both lords and merchants had on the working classes.

Bond describes the structure of the play's second half as different from the first:

> The second half looks at the first half as it were under a microscope. Then you see the magnificent fortifications of its cancer but—since we are not talking of a dying society but one that recreates itself—you also see the opposed streams: the dark satanic stream of Are becoming more powerful—the quickness of wit becoming the craftiness of his scheming (the ride to the gallows) but also the stream of opposition.[7]

This difference is important as Bond states "the second half is the reason for doing the play":

> The first half sets up a theatrical convention which was originally designed to present and justify a social attitude. The second half deconstructs this. The first half makes the atrocities of society acceptable—its mottos are "You have only yourself to blame" and "God helps those who help themselves." The second half shows the burden of this cynicism.[8]

The separation between the play's two halves is notable in production, a problem that was apparent in the 1988/9 revival. One of the keys to understanding the play's division is evident in the music, which will be further explored as a production element later in this chapter.

Another distinction evident in the play's structure recalls Anna's description of "two worlds" from *The Worlds*; a separation between the artificiality of life as lived by Lord Are, and reality, symbolized by Bob and Rose, who are desperate to ensure that Bob is not killed for a crime that he did not commit.[9] This division of artificiality from reality is captured by Bond in his parable of the child and the clock:

> The child takes the clock to bits because mummy says, "In our society, when this hand is there and that hand is there it means five o'clock. And that is a law, you must learn that, it is a convention." And if the child does not do that he will not get his meal, he will arrive late for school and his whole life will collapse. So he has got to learn how to read the clock. And so the child will get hold of the clock and take it to bits and find all these little cogs and springs inside—or little batteries and so on nowadays—and he will try and puzzle out why that is what makes the clock work. The child will be in two different worlds: one is abstract, so pure, it tells the time and the whole world obeys it. And the other is this curious mass of nuts and bolts and so on. Well, you can investigate the curious mass of nuts and bolts but that alone will not tell you what the time is.[10]

The story is appropriate in considering *Restoration* because the play places an audience in both the "pure" world of appearance and the "curious" actuality of society. According to Bond, *Restoration* should make us question why an eighteenth century society, like our own contemporary world, functions in the first place. For as Bond comments: "the fundamentals haven't changed. Only appearances have."[11]

Restoration contains thirteen characters, eight male and five female, and revolves around the action of Lord Are, an impoverished aristocrat. As a result of his poverty, Are has decided to marry Ann, the daughter of Hardache, a wealthy industrialist. Like Mrs Pinchwife, in Wycherley's *Country Wife*, Ann is consumed with desire to leave the country and visit London. Typifying her level of intelligence, Ann dons a white sheet and poses as the family spirit. In this outfit, she tries to persuade Are to take his wife to London on the pretext of pregnancy, claiming that to ensure the child will not carry a curse, the offspring needs to be born in town. Are is not concerned in the slightest by the presence of a "ghost" and, once insulted, decides to be rid of it by running it through with a rapier. On discovering the spirit to be his wife, Are skillfully transfers the blame for the murder onto his servant, Bob. Rose, Lady Are's black maidservant and also Bob's wife, discovers the truth of Ann's death, and tries but fails to obtain Bob's release. Protesting his innocence, Bob goes to his death.

In terms of humor, Lord Are is at the center of *Restoration*; an amusing character with wit, charm and a sardonic outlook on life. Comparisons have been made between Lord Are and Etherege's Dorimant, Vanburgh's Lord Foppington and Congreve's Mirabell, all of which are appropriate but limit the source of Are's comedy purely to his character. Bond would prefer that humor emerged from the play's meaning. An example of this can be found early in the play when Are, preparing to "seduce" Hardache's daughter, is confronted by Bob:

Bob. Bob sir. Or Robert Hedges.
Are. Bob, yonder is a paddock. Go and graze.
Bob. Graze sir?
Are. A country lad must know how to graze!
Bob (aside). I must learn their ways if I'm to survive—Ay sir.
Are. Then graze.
Bob (shrugs. Aside). I'll chew three stalks t' show willin'. That'll hev to doo.

Bob goes.[12]

An audience is amused by the absurdity of the situation but also, and this is a typical response to Are's character, by his biting wit. But what is significant is that Bond uses such wit to make a political point, as Katharine Worth explains.

The town/country joke, stock in trade of Restoration comedy, has here from the start an acrid, worrying quality which derives partly from the rather sinister isolation of masters and servants.[13]

The politics of Lord Are's character are further emphasized as the play progresses and an audience laughs *with* not *at* him. However, some critics failed to appreciate the political function of comedy within the context of Bond's play. G.E.H. Hughes exemplifies this misunderstanding when he comments; "Are's foppishness is meant to disgust us while Foppington's is very much there to amuse."[14] Initially, an audience should *not* be revolted by Are. Given the manipulation and cruelty Are executes in the play, Bond wants his audience to feel as guilty as the fictional character. In the 1981 production, Are's wit was similarly misunderstood. One critic commented: "Bond's humour is of the primitive, simple-minded kind that seems to please Sloane Square audiences as much as it depresses me."[15] Comedy is a political device used by Bond to demonstrate the seeming artificiality of an eighteenth century world whilst, at the same time, providing an audience with the reality of how society is organized. This notion is both confirmed and complicated by the "ghost-scene" at the end of Part One.

The episode takes place at breakfast in the Hall of Hilgay. Charged with Are's persistence, the encounter gives rise to comedy:

> Are.   My wife? What of my wife?. . . Have ye come to tell me she's to
>   join ye? I thank ye for the good news and bid ye be gone so I
>   may celebrate in peace.
> Ann.   (aside). The monster—Thy wife must flee to London. Flee!
> Are.   To London? Why?
> Ann.   She is with child. If 'tis born here 'tis forever cursed.
> Are.   Forsooth? And who will bear the expense of a London lying in?
>   Let the cow doctor child her, as he did all my family.[16]

The asides, spoken directly to the audience, are also humorous and assist in breaking any sense of "realism" which may have developed. They remind us that we are simply watching a play within the theatre. With Ann's death, which, in approach, recalls Bodice's and Fontanelle's torture of Warrington in *Lear*, Bond mingles comic technique with the grotesque. Are's murder of the "ghost" is a moment of personal insecurity—how is he to resolve the dilemma? His doubt soon passes and he recovers from the killing of "a heavy ghost." But what of the audience who have also witnessed the murder? Katharine Worth indicates that "Are is forced into unaccustomed feeling (for his own danger) and we are forced, if only for this moment, to think of the caricatured wife as a human being who can bleed."[17] Ann's death causes a momentary eclipse between the artificial world and that of reality; Are "only" attacks a ghost but the "reality" is that of killing his wife. This idea is to be developed further with Bob's assumption that *he* in fact has killed Ann. Moments after Ann's murder, Are continues with a witty observation:

> My wife. Stretched out on the floor. With a hole in her breast. Before breakfast. How is a man to put a good face on that?. . . A man cannot think with his dead wife sprawled on the carpet. And I must think—after I've tired my brains with choosing a suit for the day.[18]

A juxtaposition of comic language and situation with the murder of Lady Are is similar to what Bond will call the "aggro-effect" in connection with *The War Plays*.[19] An "aggro-effect" is a typical Bondian device, forcing us to observe the source of humor and therefore question the validity of our laughter. Unrelenting, the scene continues in this manner. As with the "innocent murder" Hatch commits in *The Sea*, the already dead Ann is stabbed again by Bob as she "chases" him round the room, carried by Are. It is a grisly moment which, like Mrs Lewis's response to Brian's corpse in *Jackets II* or Dodds and Leonard from *In The Company of Men* as they attempt to get Oldfield's corpse to sign his will, evokes strongly mixed emotion from the audience. The moment's purpose is to confuse, and therefore question, the response of an audience. Do we laugh, and if so, what are we laughing at? In a letter, Bond discusses the purpose of the play's humor:

> If I like a joke—I laugh at it—I've seen the point. But humour in the theatre is more than this—because it extends over the play and the character, so one doesnt just see the point but sees—assents to or objects to—the situation. By using laughter and tragedy (not tragi-comedy, but each mode distinct), the situation is divorced from its common description: and so an act of judgement is necessary. The writer can't impose that judgement—the spectator judges and has to accept responsibility for the judgement. The play makes the spectator declare him or herself. You see a joke—you dont understand it. The play deals with the situation that should make something funny or tragic. What Bob needs from Are is not his pardon but his wit.[20]

For Bond, comedy must always have a social purpose, reminding and confronting us with the larger issues of discrimination and injustice. So the dramatic function of the murder scene is that of defining an audience's response to the play. It does this by confronting one of its central issues; the nature of Are and the relationships of his exploitive class towards society. Seen in an amusing but also dangerous light, the upper classes are shown as manipulators of events. In a letter about *Restoration*, Bond comments on the manipulation of Are:

Lord Are seems to want to turn the whole world into an office party.
But the boss at the office party never forgets business. Really he eyes
up his party guests as the hangman eyes up his victims—who will cause
trouble, whose shirt is worth pinching. But he can do this with mania-
cal glee—because the sky has itself become the beam of the gallows.[21]

The upper classes in the play use language as a tool in their
fight for political advantage. According to Bond, language is "so
oppressive and so subtle in its form of oppression":[22]

The Restoration language is dazzled. It does not want you to listen to
the meaning. It almost wants to move so quickly that you cannot get
the meaning, you just get the dazzle. So it has to do with humour and
brilliance. It is the language of a society cunning in itself, it is the language of finance.[23]

This "dazzle" may be one of the reasons Are and other upper
class characters of Bond's are so witty. But, in the same terms,
such glamour can be a danger to society:

The language that we have now is not based on telling the truth, it is
the "wit of lies," if you like. And it is based on lying. You never call anything by its true name. I shall give you a very extreme example: what
did you call people in concentration camps? You called them pieces.
That is the language of violence—it is quite witty.[24]

Bond's intention is to abolish artificiality and "treat things as
they are."[25] Consequently, the discrepancy between the affected
language of Are and his associates with the reality of his situation, is another device which forces an audience to examine
society.

Hardache also coerces people to fit with his arrangements.
For example, his only motive in arranging the marriage
between Are and his daughter is his desire for the coal underneath Are's land. As a result of such a liaison, Hardache has
become a partial recipient of this wealth. Ann's death threatens
this plan. In order to ensure his prosperity, Hardache black-
mails Are with his knowledge of Ann's real murderer. The Parson, like the Padre of *Jackets II*, protects the aristocracy. This is
confirmed by the Parson's discussion of Lord Are with Bob at
Holme Cottage:

Lord Are is the guardian of our laws and orderer of our ways. He must
stand above all taint. Topple him from his mighty seat and Beelzebub

will walk the lanes of Hilgay. We cannot even contemplate it. Already
the methodists rant at his lordship.[26]

Direct acknowledgement of Lord Are's position by the Parson
comes in a revised version of the text written for the RSC's
1988/9 production of *Restoration*. It confirms Bond's approach,
traces of which were evident in the earlier version, that religion
as embodied by the Parson is a protective mask for class domination. The revised text, as well as showing the Parson support-
ing the upper classes, exploits this dependency to satirize what
Bond considers the church's moral shortcomings. This can be
exemplified by the following extract, typical of the hypocrisy
evident in the Parson's character: "I will call in at the church
and comfort my knees on the chancel floor. Today we have
struck a blow at the methodists."[27] Although critics of Bond's
work observe that many of his characters are only one-dimen-
sional, the Parson's character is fully developed. He understands the "function" of the working classes but is nevertheless
complacent and chooses not to be involved in struggle. The
theft of Are's silver, for example, causes Mrs Hedges to weep
and the Parson to observe her commitment to others' wealth:

> This woman learns of a lifetime of wasted labour. The cherished things
> on which she lavished her affection are gone. How will she occupy the
> time she would have devoted to cleaning them? And who is to say that
> in the hotness of pursuit fear has not triumphed over greed? Even now
> the loot may lie in the mud at the bottom of a ditch.[28]

Beneath the Parson's cynical observation of life bleeds an
underlying Marxist (and Christian) lesson on the emptiness of
material possessions. However, according to Bond, this emptiness is not to be filled by embracing God but in following the
play's maxim written by Bob, spoken and taught by the Parson:
"Man is what he knows." The Parson is happy to escape from
"truth" in alcohol but Rose, and eventually Bob, understand the
meaning contained in the phrase.

In *Restoration*, working class characters are represented in
four stages of development which can be seen as relative
degrees of enlightenment, ranging from total ignorance to
social insight. Put crudely these are a misplaced trust in the
upper classes, resignation, anarchy and understanding.

Bob is the naive, unaware servant whose trust in Are costs him his life. From the beginning of *Restoration*, Bob Hedges shows the extent of his faith: "Why sir 'tis Bob—come of age and sent up to serve as yoor man, as laid down in the history of our estate: eldest Hedges boy hev the right to serve his lord."[29] However, Bond was very concerned that Bob should not come over as a foolish figure:

> The wider implications of Bob's misplaced fidelity, of his false con-sciousness, must be made clear. It mustn't be a play about a gullible boy misled by a posh crook. . . This is important. Bob isn't stupid but his intelligence is abused.[30]

As a consequence of Are's murder of Ann, Bob is blamed and imprisoned but accepts responsibility for the death. Assured by Are that he is to get a pardon, Bob defends his master: "We accuse him we'll starve gal. Never git another job's long's we live. We jist hev to go along for the sake of appearance—like he say."[31] However, Bob's foolishness demonstrates the source of the problem—a society represented by Are. Bond has observed:

> I can imagine a version of the play in which Bob tears up the reprieve if it came—to the foot of the gallows—because it was his duty to die for his country's law and order.[32]

Lady Are's death awakes in Bob a desire to "better" himself by taking reading lessons from the Parson. In doing so, he spells out one of the play's themes: "Man is what he knows." Bob's realization that his life could have been so different, only occurs towards the end of the play and, consequently, at the end of his life. In Bond's opinion, Bob's situation represents the plight of everyman. Through this character, Bond points his accusatory finger at society:

> People do things as a result of their beliefs and opinions. Very often what they believe and think is decided not by rational thought but by the unconscious motivations of their class position. People tend to see the world for their own view of it. These things can make up much of the texture of a play—the grain in the wood.[33]

Mrs Hedges, Mrs Wilson, Gabriel, the messenger and Gaoler constitute those resigned, and therefore complacent, in life. The futility of their customary existence is made clear in meaningless tasks. For example, the cleaning of Are's silver spoons by Mrs Hedges demonstrates her attitude towards the world:

> Mother say "When yoor turn come, yoo clean 'em as good as that gal'. She bin in the churchyard twenty years. Wash 'em an set 'em an clean 'em after but ont eat off 'em once.[34]

The speech contains pangs of regret that the social system is not more equitable, but Mrs Hedges obeys the structure and, like her ancestors, is seen to be crushed as a result.

Pathetic to the extreme, but typical of how upper classes manipulate lower classes in the play, is the action of Mrs Hedges lighting the fire. At this moment, Are takes advantage of her inability to read by handing her Bob's pardon to start the fire. Mrs Hedges's illiteracy was explicitly stated in the earlier text but deleted by Bond as unnecessary in the later RSC version:

> Are.   Lookee, light a fire against my return. The day might yet be cold. Warm thy old hands at the blaze. Here is a paper to start it. (He gives her the pardons.)
>
> Mother.   Kind on him. Save me fetch the kindlin. Official. Pretty crown on top. Cut them out for Christmas decoration. (Shakes her head.) Best do what yoo're towd. Bob was learnin' to read. (Tears the papers.) Ont start that doo yoo ont git the work out the way.[35]

Mrs Hedges's regard for authority, and doing what is "right," costs her Bob's life. As Bond observes; "for the sake of justice the mother would even sacrifice her son."[36] Mrs Hedges is undoubtedly a victim, both of her own volition and the society that traps her.

The songs which Mrs Hedges sings somewhat belie her actions. "Wood Song" contains a spark of revolutionary fervor with, "All you who would resist your fate/Strike now it is already late." And in the "Legend of Good Fortune," Mrs Hedges suggests Mankind has a need to defend itself against attack by outside forces. But her words and actions do not effect change. Since the initial Royal Court production of *Restoration*, the United Kingdom had fought Argentina to protect the Falkland Islands. Bond wanted to reflect the alternative public feelings about the war and so wrote "Falkland Song," replacing the "Legend of Good Fortune," for the 1988/9 revival. This further emphasized the apathetic attitude of Mrs Hedges, and our own, through a song which mirrors the war's futility whilst, at the same time, challenging an audience to consider its own injustice. According to Bond, the character of Mrs Hedges is divided. She is at once involved in the world of Lord Are but also able to remove herself from it:

> Mrs Hedges has a folk song (Wood) because she's obviously deeply captured in the Are-dominated situation. But she also, at the Court, sang with the most revolutionary character. It is therefore a natural extension of the character to make her sing one of the most extreme statements: though you notice that it is mourning as well as defiant.[37]

Mrs Wilson is landlady at the gaol's "beer barrel." Reminiscent of several women in Bond's work, such as Mary of *Saved* and Mrs Lewis of *Jackets II*, Mrs Wilson feigns respectability to cover the inadequacy she feels as a victim of the class structure. Consequently, Mrs Wilson is obsessed with money. Everything is thought of in material terms: the door, which is broken, the beer, which is sold, and the tips given to her husband by the "better class," although even this income is uncertain. As a result of being at the financial mercy of others, Mrs Wilson has a bitter streak; "Winter coming but no one helps me with the fuel bill. . . I need a new broom. They ought to be provided by the authorities."[38] References to "a carpet upstairs," and "a few pairs of Sunday gloves" typify Mrs Wilson's illusions of a good life yet her real character emerges when she provides food for the guests. "Help yourself. (She pushes the plate further away.)"[39] In Bond's view, such individuals are not only complacent in their attitude but have been made selfish and unpleasant by society. Her instructions to the chained and imprisoned Bob: "Try not to clank dear. My head's been arguing with me all morning" is typical of her insensitive manner.[40]

Anarchy is represented by Frank. Described as the "outdoor servant," Frank understands the way society works, shown through his "Song of Learning," in which he tells of a working class enslaved for so long they understand how to "blow up your hell."[41] Frank is a radical who overturns traditional expectations. By having Frank rob Are of his silver, Bond shows him engaged in attempting to defeat society's structure: "Yer have to steal in my job if yer wanna live. Yer fetch an' carry for 'em, pick 'em up, get 'em upstairs, put 'em to bed, clean up the spew."[42] Frank's approach, of robbing the rich, holds no future for him and, by inference, anyone who would combat the world in this way. Bond sees his revolutionary instinct as admirable but analytically believes his energies are channelled in the wrong direction, attempting to reform society piecemeal instead of replacing its total structure.

Rose, the black servant and survivor, learns society's wickedness; *Restoration* closes with her determination to effect change. "Rose sees the chains in people's mouths: just as you might see their white breath on a cold day."[43] Unlike Bob, Rose understands how individuals, such as Are, have become manipulators of other people. Against accusations that she cannot recognize the world's situation, Rose believes she has an additional dimension to her understanding—her color:

> When yer black, it pays to know the law. No one can benefit from their own crime. Are killed his wife—so he loses her money. It goes back to the next of kin: her father.[44]

Rose exhibits insight throughout the play commenting for example that Frank should not be punished for stealing: "That lot can afford a bit of silver. Chriss the work they've got out of him, he deserves it."[45] She releases Frank in a move which cannot be understood by the others. Unlike them, Rose recognizes the "true" workings of human beings. This insight into the human situation is one of her characteristics. For example, in scene eight she refers to Bob as a slave who fails to recognize his enslavement: "My mother *saw* her chains, she's had marks on her wrists all her life. There are no signs on *you* till you're dead."[46] In Bond's opinion this is true of all the working class characters in *Restoration*, including Rose. But unlike the others, Rose knows her chains are there and learns from the play's action. This is clear in her final address to the audience: "I must have one hand of iron and the other of steel. There is a gentle breeze from the city. I cross the bridge and go into the streets."[47]

For Bond, the 1981 production came at a particularly appropriate time, as Wednesday July 29, 1981 saw the wedding of
Prince Charles, next in line to the British throne, to Lady Diana
Spencer. This gave Bond an opportunity to draw parallels
between his play and the Royal Wedding. In the *Guardian*
newspaper, Bond equated Are with Royalty and its manipulation of the working class:

> The wedding [of Prince Charles and Lady Diana Spencer] is a celebra-
> tion of the ruling class and therefore it is a celebration of what is irra-
> tional in society. The ruling class in this country enables exploitation to
> be done under the guise of legality. This conceals the gangsterism that
> it really is.[48]

Bond further suggested that the discrimination felt by women
in society was not simply a result of male psychology: "It is the
product of our particular authoritarian society where there is a
chain of repression from one group to another."[49]

Other contemporary events must also have been on Bond's
mind. Prior to the play's opening, street riots occurred in Brix-
ton, South London, which ended with groups of black youths
fighting the police: 279 policeman and 48 youths were injured.
There were racial riots elsewhere in London (Southall), in Liv-
erpool (Toxteth) and trouble was also reported in the cities of
Birmingham, Blackburn, Bradford, Derby, Leeds, Leicester and
Wolverhampton. Through the character of Rose, the problems
of color are addressed in the play and embodied by someone
who tries, but fails, to help Bob. For Bond some of the rioting
had its positive aspects. "I thought the racist conflict was a very
good and informed political confrontation—a rational response
to irrationality."[50] Bob is trapped in the middle of this conflict
between the two classes. According to Bond, he represents the
"typical working class Tory voter, and the play is about his
betrayal."[51] With these insights, we can connect Bond's play to
the period of political turmoil in which it was born.

The rehearsal period began in June 1981 and was, according
to Philip Davis, who played Bob, too short for much experimental work.[52] Bond, nevertheless, had a very precise idea of what
he wanted from the production and had decided that rehearsal
time was to be spent exploring the character's function in great

detail. Initiating such a process resulted in a great deal of conflict between the cast and director. Eva Griffith, who played Lady Are in the production, felt that much of the difficulty lay in Bond's inability to translate his thoughts into concrete theatre terms:

> All of us, especially Simon [Callow] had a great desire to know what Edward wanted and if he had been able to communicate that it would have been a great deal of help to him as well as us. It would be marvellous to do a play the way a writer originally conceived it. With a writer that uses words as skillfully as Bond you are bound to want those words to come across in a certain way. Then it becomes difficult to put that into terms an actor can understand.[53]

Bond's apparent failure in communicating his needs to an actor is captured by Simon Callow who created Are in the first production. In his book, *Being an Actor*, Callow describes the process in detail, both the problems he had with the role of Are and his thoughts on Bond's approach to acting.

Initially, Callow approached the role of Are "naturalistically" as, a "machiavel, a devil, a demonic Olivierian figure, best riding the stage like a colossus, eyes flashing, mouth twisted in a personal sneer."[54] Bond gradually removed this image by informing the actor that he was being too "emotional" and "sinister." This continued until Callow arrived at "his new performance:... Eighteenth-century man, genial, agreeable, reasonable, rational, with his fixed and highly satisfactory world view."[55] One difficulty Callow had in creating Are was his own conception of character. He describes the way in which he approaches a role:

> You're breaking down your own thought patterns and trying to reconstruct them into those of the character, pushing into emotional territory which may be strange and difficult for you, seeking the bodily centre of an alien being.[56]

Bond disagrees with this technique of constructing a character. In notes to *The Worlds*, Bond stated to the actors: "Judge by the situation, not by the character or his actions. They are not to look for soul, for it's a white rabbit pulled from the hat when the truth's hard to follow."[57] Rejecting Callow's Stanislavskian approach, which Bond might argue is only for the actor's benefit, Bond believes in situating character within a wider social context. In this way we see someone, such as Are, linked with society. Bond has elaborated on this idea:

> One always wants to capture the individual but to realise that, in doing so, one isn't talking about a mysterious sub-conscious but that one is talking about how that character was formed as a series of reactions with other people and the environment within which that individual is confined. To say somebody is greedy doesn't really mean very much. It could be a greedy banker or a greedy miser. That may be one thing, but suppose it's a greedy man who happens to be starving?. . . You actually have to say that starvation is a product of a particular social circumstance and greed must also be a circumstance.[58]

Bond is concerned that characters do more for an audience than simply reflect their situation:

> What art can do is mimic reality, it says, "Here's a character and it is like that person you know in the street." I am tempted to say, "Well go and look at that person on the street, why bother to come and look at that person on the stage?" There must be something art is doing and it is using that character, politics and an event in a way that is not available to the outside world.[59]

But Callow suggests that, in practice, Bond failed at developing this sense of what was required from the actor. For example, he felt Bond provided unhelpful images that did not give a "sensation." In response to the actor's request to know what music Are was like, Bond remarked: "He's like a piano being played with a stiletto knife. . . Another thing; he's like an eighteenth century carriage with a steam engine inside."[60]

Callow widens his field of attack in considering Bond's concept of acting in general:

> The actor, I think, he views with distrust and suspicion. He believes that the actor's job is simple and mechanical (say the lines, do the moves) . . . and because he has no understanding of the process of acting, he's unable to understand the difficulties, and therefore, unable to solve them. . . he understands his own plays perfectly and is always right in what he says about them. But translating what he says into acting is almost impossible.[61]

Obviously this is a subjective response to a difficult situation because what Callow considers fundamental to his craft, Bond considers self-indulgent. For example, Callow was interested in

establishing for himself the private life of Are as a member of
the Hell-Fire Club "deeply involved with rats and dead
babies."[62] Bond was not concerned with naturalizing Are in this
way. Instead he was interested in the character's dramatic and,
more importantly, political function.

A characteristic style of Bond's direction is in the suggestion
that poetic images must lie on the surface, not exist internally
and solely for the actor. His notion of directing is turning theory into practice, an approach which means poetry can become
an active vocabulary.

Davis indicates that although there was no improvisation in
rehearsals for the original production, Bond emphasized his
need for the play to explore a "non-naturalistic" approach.
There is some foreshadowing here of Bond's concept of the
"other world" emphasized in rehearsals for *Jackets II*:

> Edward was after some very strange things. Like he wanted Bob to
> make some sort of noise when he saw the ghost. In the script it was
> "eeeek" and he wanted me to do it almost verbatim. I said, "It's not
> real," and he said "It doesn't matter we are looking for a different sort
> of noise." I got an inkling he was after something that had never been
> asked of me before but I was not quite sure what it was and through
> experimenting we found something. We had a foot in both worlds. It
> was a weird noise.[63]

Bond was trying to distance Davis, and through him the audience, from a psychological reaction. Instead he wanted to
explore what Bill Gaskill, a director of the Royal Court Theatre,
intended when he described an epic theatre:

> You will find that though [the actor] will *state* the narrative clearly, he
> will often present it emotionally, and in fact what he is presenting *is*
> the emotion. Soon he gets the hang of it, and it does teach him more
> than anything else, a peculiar awareness. This awareness is the impor-
> tant thing. It doesn't matter what he wants to do in the scene, provided
> he sees what it *is* that he is doing. Most actors—certainly English
> actors—tend to present everything at once, a bit of emotion, a bit of
> character, a bit of social content, throwing it all at you in a great
> muddle.[64]

Irene Handl, who played Old Lady Are in the original production, represented the approach to acting Bond believes

redundant. Norman Tyrrell, the Parson, remarks on her playing of the character:

> I recollect some discussion going on between Edward Bond and Irene Handl. It seemed clear to me that she was going to do her act whether he liked it or not and, in the end, he manifestly gave up. In the event, she did a solo recitation, as it were, to enormous response from the front—as near a standing ovation as can be possible outside of opera—almost unbalancing the play and proving, incidentally, that Edward Bond knew what he was up to.[65]

Davis adds that, in his opinion, Handl failed to appreciate the kind of play she had committed herself to:

> It occurred to some, just before we opened, that we were in a play that might cause a violent revolution or something. Irene Handl, for example, got onto it sometime on and wished she had not done it.[66]

Despite Handl's subsequent reluctance at involving herself in the production, her performance was praised. This opens an interesting line of enquiry as to whether Bond had the right instincts about how the character was acted. The answer lies at the center of Bond's approach to his work in performance. Bond is of the opinion that anything can be made to "work" by making it "popular" to an audience. This "success" is undoubtedly what Handl achieved in her portrayal of Old Lady Are. However, we are left with the question as to whether this approach was faithful to the demands of the script, throwing the character off center and detracting from the production's tone.

Although of little help to Callow, Bond's images and metaphors were helpful to Simon Russell Beale in his playing of Are for the September 1988/9 revival of *Restoration*. Russell Beale responded favorably to Bond's ideas from the earlier production, making contact with Callow about them. In Russell Beale's opinion, much of the work had already been carried out by Callow in his creation of Are and carefully documented in *Being an Actor*, which Russell Beale had studied. But how did Bond help an actor approach the role of Are for a second time?

Bond had not taken part in any of the revival's rehearsal process at Stratford-upon-Avon. Only when the Royal Shakespeare

Company's production transferred to London (a regular policy of the RSC) opening on March 29, 1989, did Bond assist in rehearsals. During the re-rehearsal process, metaphors were just one technique Bond used. Much of the time was spent in close textual analysis, during which Bond left the first half, "mainly Are's great comic half, almost untouched."[67]

One advantage to having Bond in rehearsals is that he is able to change an approach to his text. Roger Michell indicated Bond's solution to the difficulty they experienced with the play's penultimate scene:

> The first thing he suggested was re-arranging the furniture and the scene became even more about these characters in their hermetically sealed worlds. Consequently, they found it very unnecessary to deal with each other's worlds. He took Frank's speech, about going home, and interspersed it with other bits of dialogue. So instead of being a set piece it became a splintered collection of impulses surrounded by other activities; someone crying, eating. I thought it was terrific, it really resolved that final scene for me.[68]

Although a substantial part of his participation in the revival's re-rehearsal process was textually-based, Bond did use the technique of improvisation for the Hardache scene. Beale recalls:

> When Lord Are came on and met Hardache, the scene actually exploded and we used the whole stage. I came right the way downstage which, at the Swan [Theatre in Stratford-upon-Avon] made Mrs Wilson's room more like a ballroom. The geography was completely exploded. What Edward then did was to say, "Can you and Hardache please walk round the room arm in arm during this scene." There was this wonderful Gentleman's club coziness about it. One image was used by George Smiley [from John Le Carre's novel, *Smiley's People* and a televised serial from the BBC] they walk in step and wear heavy overcoats talking about the downfall of Eastern Europe. Edward wanted that sort of feeling. He took the explosion he had unintentionally caused and exposed it even further so it became a non-naturalistic scene. . . It was a useful rehearsal tool.[69]

My view of the revival is that the RSC's production of *Restoration* at the Pit in London was successful because the play's structure was apparent. Such clarity of the play's structure may have been because Bond was present at rehearsal and able to examine incidents in a way which had not been approached for the

Stratford-upon-Avon production. Bond describes the re-
rehearsal process:

> I went through scenes and encouraged them [the actors] to reinvesti-
> gate the incidents—to open them out and use them. This worked
> because even before I got there the cast felt that they were missing the
> content of the second half. . . [The cast] were welcoming and inviting
> because R[oger] M[ichell']s work had made them so. I was able to use
> this—simply pointing to the gaps. But I didnt have the chance to really
> push the play to its definitions for the actors. . . In this respect it was
> like the play at the Court—no time.[70]

Bond's major development as director of the 1981 production was in his continued evolution of an acting style. He recognized that both classes, those represented by Are and Rose,
were to have a "mechanical" quality.

> Lord Are is like a machine, processing life so that he will remain "on
> top. . . I see the cipher-figures as little tiny mannequins, little figures
> cut out of tin and being pushed about on sticks attached to their feet,
> as in children's toy theatres.[71]

As Bond has observed: "I have to show not 'individual' psychology but 'social' psychology—that is, psychology politically determined."[72] Such an approach towards psychology is an important aspect of Bond's form of theatre. In notebooks for the
play, he comments on the significance of character and story,
major components of Brecht's concept of Epic theatre which
influenced Bond in this production:

> To tell a story. The actor should not try to experience what its like to
> be a character. He should take pleasure in telling the story. As a story-
> teller he imitates the character about which he is telling—from time to
> time he imitates him almost rudely, almost with a wink, as if to say: this
> is the guy exactly.[73]

As Philip Roberts indicates: "This notion of the divorce at times
between the actor and the character is deployed to acutely
comic ends.[74] Are's asides, and use of direct address, are ways
of separating *Restoration* from "real" life enhancing a main
characteristic of Bond's work: a play's ability to comment on
itself.

Within the context of traditional Restoration drama, another "alienation" technique, used in both text and production, is that Rose's skin is black. Her color is used as a discriminating force. Are refers to Rose as a "black slut," and Ann, convinced of her magical powers, asks "Can you do voodoo?. . . It comes naturally to you people."[75] Even Mrs Hedges mentions her color: "Black cow gives milk same as white cow. They say black the grate an' the fire burn better."[76] In a similar way to Shakespeare's Othello, Rose is vulnerable because of her color, but in *Restoration* Bond inverts this vulnerability, turning it into an advantage. By marrying a white man, Rose has already violated social norms and demonstrated her dismissal of expected conventions. Combined with her strength as an individual, Rose's lack of fear enables her to speak out against Lord Are, in contrast to those of a similar status, such as Bob, who respect and maintain the social equilibrium.

It should be clarified that the circumstances surrounding the two productions of *Restoration* in 1981 and 1988/9 were very distinctive, making assessment of their respective qualities problematic. In 1981, Bond had control over elements of the production, design, lighting, casting, that were denied him at the Royal Shakespeare Company as he was only present in the role of advisor. But the need to have Bond in the rehearsal room seems to suggest that his practical interpretation of the play is required. By juxtaposing the various elements from the 1981 and 1989 productions of *Restoration*, it is possible to demonstrate the significance of Bond's contribution to the overall process.

Bond's stylistic interpretation of *Restoration* for the original 1981 production was, customarily, simple. One critic correctly indicates the significance of Bond's directorial choices:

> Bond is a master of stage imagery. The look of his stage—its customary bareness, its few symbolic objects—is an important means for him of moving easily between public and private worlds and of heightening and focussing our attention, to bring us further into the mental landscape inhabited by his characters. . . Lighting, groupings, spatial arrangements, function in Bond's plays as in Beckett's, with great poetic economy, for a subtle variety of dramatic purposes.[77]

This comment is in sharp contrast to David L. Hirst's assumption that: "Unlike Beckett, for example, Bond is a writer who does not have a set idea of how his plays are to be done."[78] Numerous stage directions and the control Bond requires as a director invalidates this comment. Bond's attention to detail can be exemplified by specifications for the set of *Restoration*, the costumes and, more significantly, the production's music.

Hayden Griffin's and Gemma Jackson's setting for the 1981 production was sparse and functional. One example is the first scene in Lord Are's Park, defined by cut-out trees lowered from the flies. No attempt was made at trying to capture a sense of reality. Griffin believes Bond's "secret" in assisting designers is suggesting a simplicity which, in itself, is extremely complex:

> Bond is visually incredibly clear about what he wants and, I believe, knows what he wants to see when he writes. The problems directors have with him is that he does know what he has visualized. Edward is a great man of the theatre and knows that if you give the audience one simple visual idea then their imagination will start to pour out of their heads. An example of this would be *The Pope's Wedding*; "The boys come on stage. There is an apple. It is summer." This is one of the greatest stage directions in the whole of British theatre. What he is saying is that if you give the audience three or four contact points, their imagination will draw the picture.[79]

Griffin describes the set for *Restoration* as awkward not because of any deficiency but simply because it proved difficult to "fly" due to its peculiar angle. He also designed costumes which visually assisted in dividing the upper from lower classes. Are wore resplendent period dress whilst his wife, played by Eva Griffith, was dressed in "the most beautiful costumes with the most lurid colours and bows in all the wrong places."[80] This provided a contrast to the working class; for example, Debbie Bishop, as Rose, wore a simple, plain dress and headscarf. Bond's idea about costume is that what is worn is significant and should not limit or define their character:

> When we think of clothes as being symbolic: then they impose a social posture. The suits presidents wear in office, the leisure gear they wear on a golf-course. So do you wear clothes for the place? No—the red alert may happen on the golf-course. The point in a play is that you have to choose the red alerts—and so that the character would wear "x"

isnt necessary to the situation. To dress the character—in a way which
totally assumes the character as given—is a mistake.[81]

David Field's setting for the 1988/9 production was predomi-
nantly white, with set pieces, such as the tree in the first scene,
being brought on stage only for that scene. Michael Coveney
makes a significant comment on this choice in his review of the
play for the *Financial Times*:

> Roger Michell lays out the play cleanly on a bright white set designed
> by David Fielding and, as in all the best Bond productions, makes con-
> crete the images in space.[82]

Michell has observed that in directing this play, "You find out
what each object means and you cut away until you just have
these objects":

> The spoon scene for example. You have a tray of spoons which repre-
> sent the bars in the old woman's life. So you have to find the right
> prop to tell that story. We took the actress to Blenheim Palace and we
> met a butler who taught her how an eighteenth century woman would
> polish spoons. His attitude was extraordinarily similar to her's.[83]

The production was "dazzlingly lit by Rick Fisher, as merciless
as the impartial sun that Lord Are worships."[84] Michell wanted
the lighting to be "as clean and as simple as possible without
straying into naturalism."[85] At Stratford, Fisher introduced the
idea of fluorescent tubes, lowered from the flies, for the scenes
in the prison but, because of the technical resources of the Pit
in London, this effect was abandoned when the production
transferred. In performance this lighting gave the scenes an
oppressive, almost surreal quality.

Like Bond's use of a public soliloquy in *The Worlds*, the songs
in both *Restoration* and *Jackets* aim to remove an audience from
the fabricated world of fictional individuals, allowing the characters to step outside themselves and comment on their situation. There are sixteen songs in *Restoration*: one prior to the
play, ten at the end of scenes and five in the middle of the
action. For Bond, songs are "culturally disciplined forms of
weeping—or laughing—as well as stating (usually) simple philos-
ophies: the passing of seasons and the nature of accidents."[86] It

has been observed that the songs are of three "types," and these categories make it useful in considering their function:

> Bond on occasions makes his actors come out of character for the songs themselves. On other occasions, they remain within character. Elsewhere they may begin in character but then, during the course of the song, produce views which are deliberately not compatible with the established ways of proceeding.[87]

It is unnecessary to classify each of the songs but it may be helpful to give examples and suggest the purpose of each group.

Song is reserved exclusively for the working class in *Restoration*. According to Katharine Worth, in song they gain the articulacy they lack in that world.[88] This is true of Frank's "Song of Learning." With greater clarity of thought and expression than he would possess in "real" life, Frank assesses and comments on the working class situation. The song's value lies in the communication to an audience of a class position, puncturing dismissive notions that they are out of context.[89] At the end of scene one, Bob sings to Rose in a ballad which, according to Worth, is "not one of the most successful; on the whole, the more aggressive punchy lyrics work best."[90] "Roses" is designed as an outpouring of Bob's emotion and is deliberately naive in the extreme. Here, Bond uses music to establish Bob's innocence in his understanding of the world.

"Wood Song" is an example of a song beginning in character and ending by commenting on the situation. It represents perhaps the most striking use of music in *Restoration* as the song seems to be part of the play's action and very quickly becomes a device which forces the spectators to remove themselves from the play. Bond comments on the overall use of music in the play as an "alienation" device:

> I wanted to integrate the sequence of music into the story: giving it privileges but not making it all-powerful (as if the audiences were visiting a museum of the past).[91]

Bond sees it as his moral responsibility as a writer to ensure that his songs produce a different response in an audience.

Nicholas de Jongh, theatre critic of the *Guardian*, complained that the 1988/9 production "missed the chance of locating the play in surreal or expressionistic territory."[92] My impression of *Restoration* is that such settings would be wholly inappropriate. Bond's intention is to demonstrate the timelessness of class exploitation using the conventions of eighteenth century drama for his own artistic purposes. In the next play he would work on professionally at the National Theatre, *Summer*, Bond would reveal an ability to use another dramatic style—naturalism.

Notes

1 Edward Bond, *Restoration* and *The Cat* (London: Methuen, 1982) 5.

2 Edward Bond, interview with Stephanie Buschmann, 2 October 1987.

3 Charles Spencer, *New Standard* 23 July 1981: 25.

4 Michael Billington, *Guardian* 22 July 1981: 12.

5 Edward Bond, letter to author, 10 February 1990.

6 G.E.H. Hughes, "Edward Bond's 'Restoration'" *Critical Quarterly* 25 (4) 1983: 77/8.

7 Edward Bond, letter to author, 10 February 1990.

8 Edward Bond, letter to Philomena Matheson, 5 December 1989.

9 Edward Bond, *The Worlds with The Activists Papers* (London: Methuen, 1980) 77.

10 Edward Bond, interview with Stephanie Buschmann, 2 October 1987.

11 Edward Bond quoted in "The Search for Epic Drama: Edward Bond's Recent Work," by Philip Roberts, *Modern Drama* 24 (4) 1981: 466.

12 Bond *Restoration* and *The Cat* 10.

13 Katharine Worth, "Bond's 'Restoration'" *Modern Drama* 24 (4) 1981: 480.

14 Hughes 78.

15 Kenneth Hurren, *What's On In London* July 1981.

16 Bond *Restoration* and *The Cat* 10.

17 Worth "Bond's 'Restoration'" 486.

18 Bond's *Restoration* and *The Cat* 44.

19 "Aggro-Effects" are described in Chapter 5.

20 Edward Bond, letter to Philomena Matheson, 19 February 1990.

21 Edward Bond, letter to Philomena Matheson, 5 December 1989.

22 Edward Bond quoted in *Guardian* 31 July 1981: 10.

23 Edward Bond quoted in *Guardian* 31 July 1981: 10.

24 Edward Bond, interview, with Stephanie Buschmann, 2 October 1987.

25 Edward Bond, letter to Margaret Eddershaw, 3 February 1990.

26 Edward Bond, *Restoration* (London: Methuen, 1988) 28.

27 Bond *Restoration* 29.

28 Bond *Restoration* 16.

29 Bond *Restoration* and *The Cat* 10.

30 Edward Bond quoted in *Modern Drama* 24 (4) 1981: 468.

31 Bond *Restoration* and *The Cat* 57.

32 Edward Bond, letter to author, 10 February 1990.

33 Edward Bond quoted in *Modern Drama* 468.

34 Bond *Restoration* and *The Cat* 28.

35 Bond *Restoration* and *The Cat* 89.

36 Edward Bond, letter to Philomena Matheson, 5 December 1989.

37 Edward Bond, letter to author, 10 February 1990.

38 Bond *Restoration* 28/9.

39 Bond *Restoration* and *The Cat* 71.

40 Bond *Restoration* and *The Cat* 71.

41 Bond *Restoration* and *The Cat* 20.

42 Bond *Restoration* and *The Cat* 33.

43 Edward Bond, letter to Philomena Matheson, 5 December 1989.

44 Bond *Restoration* and *The Cat* 64.

45 Bond *Restoration* and *The Cat* 33.

46 Bond *Restoration* and *The Cat* 78.

47 Bond *Restoration* and *The Cat* 100.

48 Bond quoted in *Guardian*.

49 Bond quoted in *Guardian.*

50 Bond quoted in *Guardian.*

51 Bond quoted in *Guardian.*

52 Philip Davis, personal interview, 29 January 1990.

53 Eva Griffith, personal interview, 31 January 1990.

54 Simon Callow, *Being an Actor* (New York: Grove Press, 1988) 165.

55 Callow 165.

56 Callow 135.

57 Edward Bond quoted in "Rehearsing Optimism," by Jane Bryce *Leveller* 60, July 1981: 18/19.

58 Edward Bond, interview with Nick Philippou, undated.

59 Edward Bond, personal interview, 14 December 1989.

60 Callow 134.

61 Callow 133/4.

62 Callow 165.

63 Philip Davis, personal interview, 28 January 1990.

64 William Gaskill, "Brecht in Britain in *Theatre at Work* ed., Charles Marowitz and Simon Trussler (London: Methuen, 1967) 126.

65 Norman Tyrrell, letter to author, 5 February 1990.

66 Philip Davis, personal interview, 29 January 1990.

67 Simon Russell Beale, personal interview, 5 February 1990.

68 Roger Michell, personal interview, 4 April 1990.

69 Simon Russell Beale, personal interview, 5 February 1990.

70 Edward Bond, letter to author, 10 February 1990.

71 Bond quoted in *Modern Drama* 469.

72 Bond quoted in *Modern Drama* 469 & 470.

73 Bond quoted in *Modern Drama* 467.

74 Philip Roberts in *Modern Drama* 467.

75 Bond *Restoration* and *The Cat* 74 and 24/5.

76 Bond *Restoration* and *The Cat* 18.

77 Katharine J. Worth, "Edward Bond" in *Essays on Contemporary British Drama* (Munich: Heuber, 1981) 210.

78 David L. Hirst, *Edward Bond* (London: Macmillan, 1985) 162.

79 Hayden Griffin, personal interview, 21 February 1990.

80 Eva Griffith, personal interview, 31 January 1990.

81 Edward Bond, letter to author, 23 March 1990.

82 Michael Coveney, *Financial Times*, 14 September 1988: 23.

83 Roger Michell, personal interview, 4 April 1990.

84 Martin Hoyle, *Financial Times*, 31 March 1989: 23.

85 Roger Michell, personal interview, 4 April 1990.

86 Edward Bond, letter to author, 10 February 1990.

87 Philip Roberts in *Modern Drama* 472.

88 Worth "Bond's 'Restoration,'" 483.

89 Douglas Orgill, *Daily Express* 22 July 1981: 3.

90 Worth "Bond's 'Restoration,'" 483.

91 Edward Bond, letter to author, 10 February 1990.

92 Nicholas de Jongh, *Guardian* 31 March 1989: 28.

Chapter Four

Summer

Summer is a relatively short play, lasting less than two hours in the theatre, continuing Bond's essentially Marxist exploration of life. In the play Marthe, a dying woman, confronts Xenia, a former resident of the island, with the past, making her assume responsibility for her personal actions. Bond shows the impact of this process on several characters within the dramatic context of the play, including Marthe's son David, Ann—Xenia's daughter—and their possible child.

Bond's repertory production of *Summer* opened in the Cottesloe at the National Theatre on January 27, 1982 and closed June 19 during which time it received sixty performances. The play obtained a mixed critical response ranging from the accusation that Bond was a "tedious embarrassment" to the belief that *Summer* puts him back in his rightful place, in the very forefront of our living dramatists.[1] Though stylistically different from *The Woman*, *The Worlds* and *Restoration*, *Summer* provided another opportunity for Bond to develop a consistent methodology for actors. David Ryall, the actor who played Hemmel in this production, described the work this way: "Bond wanted the acting to be pure and unemotionally charged, practically and logically argued, so you can see the question he is putting."[2] Before exploring the physical and directorial aspects of the production, it is useful to consider the evolution of the play's dramatic narrative.

From the beginning of Bond's preliminary notes for the play in September 1980, it is abundantly clear that his intention was to explore the lives of "ordinary" people:

> A possible method. Let the first section be normal. About daily things and daily complexities involving the holidaying Mrs X (Xenia), the dying Marthe and the Y(oung) C(ouple). Then go to the Island so that

the first section meets its counterpart, its illumination—involving the
visit of the CCIM (Concentration Camp Island Man)—Mrs X's shadow.
Then a final section which joins the two and draws the lesson and in
which Marthe dies . . . I want a process that will reveal a process.[3]

By the middle of November 1980, as a result of his growing
understanding about how the play should operate, Bond con-
cluded his notebooks with an analysis of the different "worlds"
inhabited by his characters:

The worlds of the daily activity—preparing food, eating, cleaning. . .
The world of discussion—that is, the reflective ideas that make sense of
the lives that the characters have led. . . The world of the drama—Xenia
against Marthe.[4]

The play is written for performance by three actresses and
two actors. (In Bond's National Theatre production, Yvonne
Bryceland appeared as Marthe, Anna Massey as Xenia, Eleanor
David as Ann, David Ryall as the German and the character of
David was played by David Yelland.) The play consists of seven
scenes, set in an unnamed seaside holiday resort in Eastern
Europe, where Xenia, a former resident of the islands, whose
family owned the land during the Second World War, and her
daughter, Ann, have returned for their vacation. Marthe, a former family servant, continues to live in the house and is dying
from a reticulosis, a blood disorder. She is cared for by her son,
David, the local doctor. During the play Ann learns how Marthe
was held captive because of the apparent murder of two German soldiers and that Marthe alone, not the other islanders
imprisoned with her, was freed by her mother's intervention.
At the end of the war, Xenia had been rescued by British
troops, later marrying the commanding officer, and Marthe had
given evidence against Xenia's father, who was subsequently
imprisoned and died.

Scene four is crucial to an understanding of the play because
it juxtaposes four generations caught up in, and affected by, the
play's action. The past is represented by an ageing German visi-
tor and ex-guard from the prison camps which had been
erected on the islands during the war. Xenia, middle-aged, is
representative of the past in the present. David and Ann, repre-

senting the future-present, are young lovers who learn life is hard and in need of change. In this respect the pair recall some of Bond's other young couples, for example, Pam and Len in *Saved*, Rose and Willy in *The Sea*, Bob and Rose in *Restoration*. The fourth generation, the future, the child that may be in Ann's womb, waits to be born.

It is in this scene that Xenia finds that, as a child, she was a silent symbol of class and racial superiority to the German army, a "beautiful girl in white," and in her own way as guilty and as responsible as the man she so obviously dislikes.[5] As a result, Bond demonstrates how, in his opinion, there are only two main social groups in the play; the oppressors (Xenia and the German) and the oppressed (Marthe and David). Ann finds herself in the middle between these two groups, learning and understanding "what people do in this world."[6]

The conclusion of *Summer* sees Xenia leaving for a hotel. While Marthe sleeps, the former German guard brings a floral tribute to Xenia and a letter protesting his innocence over his past actions. Marthe dies in her sleep and the play ends with Ann and David drinking coffee and talking about the future. However, Bond warns that discussion alone is not the answer: ". . . they must be active: they are *creating* an understanding, and this must be produced through *action*, not passive contemplation."[7]

It has been said that the play represents a new departure for Edward Bond, the work being seen as "naturalistic" in both form and style.[8] In a sense this is true; an audience enters a world populated by characters who, through their seemingly idle conversation, uncover many of Bond's fundamental political concerns: the impossibility of changing the world through kindness, the threat of war as an annihilating force, the inescapable guilt of Xenia and the German representing those who take society at face value and do nothing to change it. Bond, in taped correspondence, comments on "naturalism":

My plays are not naturalistic. They take what is natural but they are highly artificial. For example, the language of my plays. I am not trying to get the appearance of naturalism.[9]

Before I consider the political devices of *Summer*, it is necessary
to penetrate this myth of "naturalism" in which the play seems
to be enveloped.

Chekhov and Ibsen are two dramatists whose influences are
said to be evident in *Summer*. David L. Hirst, in his book on
Bond's work, makes a series of observations about Ibsen and
Bond: the arrest and imprisonment of Ann's grandfather in
Summer parallels the disgrace of Old Ekdal in *The Wild Duck*,
the influence of past events on the present is similar to *Ghosts*
and the entire play reflects "the gloom-laden environment of
Rosmersholm."[10] Any discussion of *Summer* must acknowledge
the influence of Chekhov and Ibsen but, as Hirst's study
emphasizes, Bond only establishes this "naturalistic" framework
in order to destroy it. Bond sees a parallel with Ibsen, but
demonstrates how, in his opinion, *Summer* moves on from that
tradition:

> A German director who was directing *Summer* wrote to me and said
> that he liked the play and wanted to direct it but had a few problems.
> One of the problems he told me was this: In scene three of the play,
> Xenia and Marthe are talking about the past and saying how one saved
> the other from a concentration camp. The director said that told every-
> thing. Then you get to the next scene between the two women, which
> is at night, and there has to be some revelation. Now I know what he
> means because if you take a play by Ibsen . . . you never arrive at any
> determinant or motive for human action. And therefore no real under-
> standing of what people in the play are involved in. They are shown
> coping with their problem in a certain way but they are not shown
> understanding their problem.[11]

As Roberts pointed out, "What *Summer* attempts is the analysis
of *historical* pattern focused through the ordinary, the cumula-
tive making of *history* through daily lives."[12] (My emphases).
This is one of the ways in which the play is fundamentally political and different from the work of the "naturalists." Certainly
Chekhov was concerned about society's influence on the individual in as much as it affected character. But in this play Bond
permits us to witness a complicated historical web of relationships, emphasizing their social dimension in the hope that an
audience will leave the theatre with a greater sense of social
understanding. For example, Xenia represents the business-
owning upper class and Marthe the oppressed lower class

exploited by Xenia. This discrepancy makes the confrontation between the two women inevitable. Unlike the "naturalists," Bond is not content with simply staging a problem; instead he tackles the fundamental problem of living in a capitalist world and shows a possible solution. Bond believes that any political action must begin with the daily activities of life, and thus chooses to dramatize the everyday. This cannot be confused with being purely "naturalistic."

Part of dramatizing the "ordinary" aspects of life is dealing with its cessation. In his notebooks, Bond comments:

> Often in plays (among them mine) people are trying to stay alive—they are struggling with death not death from sickness, but political or legal death. In this play I ought to ask, given that you won't be killed tomorrow, what will you live for?[13]

Another political function of *Summer* is to show Marthe's death as useful, not in order to create a fully developed character, but to demonstrate there is some hope for others in society. Towards the end of the play, Marthe has a speech in which she states "I die so that you might live."[14] Bond has argued that her death is not an empty gesture, or simply a reflection of life, but one serving as an example to the audience.[15] Consequently, Bond has little time for drama which concludes that life is meaningless. According to Bond, those are plays in which there is little substance to the story. For example, he maintains that Ibsen, "appears as a revolutionary dramatist but was a radical conservative":

> He increasingly turns the social relationships he writes about (making drama from the tensions which are breaking the old social relationships) into mysticism or the frankly occult. . . The famous stage as a room with the fourth wall missing is really a coffin with the lid off.[16]

An attack is also launched on writers like Beckett who, Bond maintains, are irresponsible in not providing us with a guide as to how to reorganize society:

> It is as if Beckett told us to be comforted because in the lungs of a corpse there is still a pocket of air. What use is that to the living? What teaching is that for the young?[17]

If *Summer* can thus be seen as a play beyond the boundaries of "naturalism," we need to examine those aspects which make it a political drama. Chiefly, this can be done by assessing the functions of the major characters—Xenia, Marthe, the German, David and Ann—within the play.

From his earliest planning of *Summer*, Bond considered Xenia an "outsider," different from Marthe and David. Everything about her reflects a class remote from everyday realities of life on the islands; her clothes, speech and manner reveal a woman experiencing a very different view of the world from Marthe. Xenia's language contains the sardonic snobbery of many upper class individuals; the "hideous new hotel," the "dreadful holiday camp" and the fear of bathing in water potentially contaminated by trash from hotel litter.[18]

One way of emphasizing Xenia's character is her reliance on external appearances, such as through her clothes. This is a familiar motif in Bond's work, echoing Mrs Rafi's curtain material in *The Sea* and the stolen clothes at the beginning of *Jackets II*. As soon as she steps ashore, Xenia cannot find a key that fits her cases. In this way, Bond emphasizes her awkwardness at being there. Despite David's offer of lending Xenia some of Marthe's or Ann's clothes, Xenia insists she needs her own: "I like to feel at home in this house—unpack my things and hang them in their place. Now there's all this muddle."[19] Xenia finds comfort in her appearance, almost as if she needs this orderliness in order to continue living.

Summer is governed by death, represented by the dying Marthe and by Xenia who, according to Bond, is already dead. Bond, in a letter to a student, describes Xenia as a "ghost":

> Xenia sells and wears beautiful clothes because she wishes to disguise her own death. If you like, Xenia was killed when she went to the island to rescue Marthe.[20]

This is not an unusual concept for Bond, who often dramatizes the "dead-living" through characters drawn from the "establishment." Such characters as the King, in the first half of *Lear*, or the Officer, in *Jackets II*, are actually agents of death for society. Linked with death through the war on the islands, Xenia now runs a "fashionable" boutique for clientele of "good taste." For

Bond, it is the fact that her political outlook is wholly immovable, lifeless, which dominates her role: "What do I mean by dead? Dead to all humane, political conscious purposes. . . the trouble with Xenia is that she is dead and not in her coffin."[21] Xenia also comes across as a frivolous figure. A conversation with David about the gravity of Marthe's illness can be used as an example:

David.	She has a reticulosis.
Xenia.	What's that? Please don't confuse me with medical jargon.
David.	It's a disease of the lymphatic glands.
Xenia.	Is it serious?
David.	Yes, it's terminal.
Xenia.	But she'll get better?[22]

Xenia thus emerges as a well-meaning character whose perception of the world is selective and consequently fails to be truthful. Further examples of this tendency occur in scene four where Xenia meets the German. The scene also shows a clash between different views of past in the present, and reveals the humor that we can find in Xenia's character. These incidents include the picnic lunch she has prepared for her gruesome visit, her reluctance at sharing the sandwich and finally her desire to escape from the island, anxiously pursued by the German hoping to obtain forgiveness.

Xenia is forced to recognize that she belongs to a class that made death-camps possible during the war, but might defend her position with an argument Bond considers as only too prevalent in our society: "Xenia would say that the exploiters gave them compensation and anyway they needed to be led."[23] Her annual visits to the islands are a way of demonstrating lingering vestiges of power, authority and philanthropy. They are the actions of an insecure and unwanted woman wishing to show political dominance in the face of a changed world. The responsibility lies with Ann to "think" about these different points of view and arrive at a conclusion as to how the world should work.

Hemmel, the German, exists to demonstrate how responsiblity for the war crimes is also shared by Xenia. Bond describes him as, "Not a big fish. Did what he was told without questions other than about his pay, accommodation and food."[24] His manner is blunt and straightforward, endowed with an innocence contradictory to his situation: "This wasn't a concentration camp. We were private soldiers: not officers, not Gestapo, not guilty."[25] Having said this, he then describes the many atrocities committed in the camps, including the exhumation of bodies and their re-burial at sea:

> We stood guard while the prisoners dug and carried. Such stench. Can you imagine? For three days. The bodies were thrown into the sea. But there is no tide. The bodies won't go away. The sea will not take them. It is as if it was against us. They floated round the island.[26]

The German's description of such horrific incidents, his calm recounting of them as Xenia eats her lunch, are intended to provoke a curious mixture of emotions for an audience.

The German represents everything Bond despises. Hemmel's attitude is the opposite of Bond's yet akin to that of Xenia who may pretend to be liberal, but is actually "inextricably entangled in responsibility" by having been a symbol of hope for the Germans.[27] Bond indicates that Xenia's view "cannot protect us against concentration camp island men—*but more*, that it is responsible for them: they are produced by the 'Xenia' society."[28] Consequently, Xenia's refusal to accept Hemmel's opinion is actually a fear of sharing his point of view. This view is found in a speech towards the end of the fourth scene:

> Men are animals. We can't be trusted with another man's wife or his money. Not even with our own daughters. No one's safe on our streets at night. If we don't get our fodder we whine. . . The animal wants to be on top.[29]

Hemmel emphasizes a further contradiction between the calm outer shell of *Summer* and the savagery of its incidents. He describes the reactions of camp officials to the disposal of corpses: "The public address system played music to keep spirits high. We came with marches and left with waltzes."[30]

Unlike Xenia, Marthe is not tied to a past of superiority. Like many characters in Bond's plays, for example Hatch in *The Sea* and Brian Tebham in *Jackets II*, Marthe represents those who have suffered at the mercy of people like Mrs Rafi and the officer. From the beginning of Xenia's and Marthe's relationship, Marthe has been constant in her dislike of Xenia and her family. Such feelings are evident in Marthe's testimony against Xenia's father at his trial. Marthe states: "I described how he lived. The parties and gambling. Many in the court had starved. It was dangerous to live in your father's world."[31]

Bond describes Marthe as a "woman who speaks the truth," recalling Ismene in *The Woman*.[32] Rejecting what society might label as "expected loyalties," Marthe lashes out at Xenia and all she represents. Such a conflict manifests itself in scene three, where both Xenia and Marthe tell Ann the circumstances surrounding Marthe's captivity and release: "When I told them the name of the woman I worked for she said 'If I could live to spit in her face' and spat in the dirt."[33] This episode is recalled later in scene five where Marthe spits at Xenia, not out of bitterness or resentment caused by her own medical condition, but to satisfy and resolve the anger caused through the fundamental class divisions between them. Hence Marthe's expression, "It's gone," at the end of the scene, indicates the final release of the old woman from her anger. This is a concept not understood by Xenia, who leaves immediately for a hotel. In a letter, Bond has stated that he believes Marthe's action of spitting at Xenia "to be like a kiss: an act of kindness."

> [It is] because Xenia is dead (and the actress playing her should play like a corpse in the latest fashionable clothes) and she needs to be told that she is making her own, private world a coffin—just as her "culture" once made Europe a graveyard. Its as if Xenia was a ghost that needed to be laid to rest by the spit.[34]

The incident clouding the entirety of *Summer* is Marthe's impending death. Finding herself in such circumstances, Marthe is unafraid of saying and acting out a philosophy of life which others may only think about. For example, she concludes the play with a strong warning to Ann: "Don't give yourself to your enemies or neglect anyone in need. Fight. But in the end death is a friend who brings a gift: life."[35] Marthe has adopted this resolute approach in her own life, a refusal to surrender to Xenia or what she represents. However Bond does not wish to trivialize her death by making it the play's centerpiece and so allows the climax of *Summer* to occur with the women's fight in scene five. Bond believes Marthe's death should occur matter-of-factly, "as if she laid the table for their breakfast. Sat. Died. They came and sat at the table and ate. They found that she was dead."[36] Bond is not suggesting in *Summer* that death is unimportant. Rather, he shows the repercussions of Marthe's death on Xenia, whose insecurities are clear when she asks Marthe, "Shall I come here when you're dead?" and to David and Ann who must continue with their lives.[37]

David and Ann need to be perceived both as individuals and jointly because, despite Ann's reluctance at the beginning, they maintain a relationship throughout the play and consequently both of them lend a special weight to the notion of a "new" world.

According to his mother, David is "young and thoughtless" although he appears both mature and responsible.[38] We learn of two contrasting sides to his nature. In material terms, he is realistic and unskeptical of his medical work. For example, in scene two, David gives a detailed account of his mother's illness, delivered with clinical precision, without a trace of emotion. But David also has a poetic view of romantic love. At the end of the fourth scene, David expresses his feelings towards Ann:

> We'll sleep together every night till you go away. I will plant a great treasure of seed in you to carry abroad to your country. There you will bear a child. The child and that pine are the only things we can give to my mother—or all who die.[39]

In this speech, David helps create a vision of the next generation. The quotation which David repeats early in the play is of Achilles's words to Priam, spoken as the old man collects his son's body; "That is the fate gods give wretched men, to suffer while they are free from care."[40] David's view is both an acceptance of past and present and a belief in the future. It unites his seemingly contradictory nature. Ann's initial refusal of David's advances and her subsequent reversal of this decision, provide humor and also expresses a spirit of optimism. Her quotation from Goethe represents this hopeful outlook. The speech comes when Ann and David are about to climb aboard a boat leaving the islands for the mainland:

The gods love the widespread races of happy men and willingly lengthen the days of his fleeting life, to share with him the joyful view from their unchanging stay, for a brief span of time.[41]

It captures the possibility of change, both for them and David's child which may grow, subsequently, in her womb. She represents Bond's hope for humanity in an almost bleak world. Bond suggests that the audience "ought to want to cheer!" when David, having made love to Ann, says "The island is sacred to us."[42] Their lovemaking, coupled with Marthe's certain death, is not irresponsible despite its apparent insensitivity. Such a disjunction contains the essence of Bond's vision. David's speech, towards the end of scene four, suggests that death strengthens life:

Death creates desire. Lust. The stupid think that's perverse. No. Lust isn't drawn to death. When life sees death it becomes strong itself, it *will* be strong.[43]

After this scene, Ann and David take on a dramatic function similar to that of Rose and Willy of *The Sea*, and Ismene and the Dark Man in *The Woman*. They represent a "new age"; a force which, for Bond, "converts the irrational and sense of death to the rational and vital":[44]

And so the island belongs to David and Ann. But they can't inherit it from Marthe: they must also struggle. So they say, we will fall in love and then part. And in this final scene they dare each other to accept this challenge—and they accept it.[45]

Max Stafford-Clark, artistic director of the Royal Court Theatre in 1982, has commented that *Summer* should have been staged at the Royal Court.[46] Peter Hall, then director of the National Theatre, admits that "in a way I think *Summer* was a sort of Royal Court play."[47] Bond suggests the play was intended for the National Theatre where he was to direct it. One of the reasons Bond wanted to direct *Summer* was to have control over the various elements of the production, such as the poster, program and acting style, in addition to the scenic elements. Having Bond as director at the National Theatre was welcomed by Hall and the administration. Hall recalls, "I like the play, I thought it would be interesting in the space at the

Cottesloe. With *The Woman*, Edward had proved he could direct."[48]

The picture on the program for the National Theatre production, directed by Bond, was a reduced, paler version of the poster. It contained the four strongest elements of the play—sun, sea, rocks and land, the most dominant of these being the setting, or rising, sun which throws its rays out across the water. It is, intentionally, reminiscent of Marthe's speech about the sun's power of attraction. The rays of the sun penetrate the entire play. Lizards bathe in it, Hemmel associates sunlight with Xenia's temper, Marthe speaks kindly of the sun to Xenia, David complains it makes everything too hot. In a related way the German reiterates the idea of light in revealing that Xenia was dressed in white as a young child. This notion of brightness was transmitted in Bond's production through the lighting, which was particularly harsh in the daylight scenes. Brightness contrasted with the costumes which, with the exception of Ann's and occasionally Marthe's, were dark in color.

Underlining this contrast, there are a number of occasions when darkness is mentioned or implied. "I dreamed I went to sleep and in the night a door banged in the wind," Marthe says to Ann in scene six. Many important scenes also occur at night: Xenia is told of Marthe's illness at night, the argument between Xenia and Marthe also occurs in the evening. David, in the penultimate scene of the play, combines both these images of light and dark: "All things under the sun throw a shadow. Your mother throws hers towards the light."[49] Darkness, like the sea, is often connected with death. For example, Xenia unites a number of images when she tells Marthe about her father's capture: "I should have drowned myself when they took him away. Gone down the rocks in the dark and slipped into the sea."[50]

Hemmel observes, "rocks are dangerous," and they are in *Summer*. They are either used to entomb the living, evoking resonances of *Antigone* and *The Woman*, or represent a past world from which none of the characters can escape:

> Look at the fossils and veins of quartz and bullet marks in the rock. . .
> There was blood on the ground—but there was blood on all the rocks
> on the island and on the walls of the rooms.[51]

Quite often, these elements overlap as with the sea and rock. Bond uses water as a corrosive force, a vehicle of change. For example, Xenia comments, "Once those islands were one piece of *rock*. Then the *sea* tore them in two."[52] (my emphases.) The sea is at its most prominent when Hemmel describes the disposal of corpses during the war. His speech is full of vivid imagery connected with the water and its rejection of death: "A dead woman clutched a child in the crook of her arm and floated on top of the sea as if she held the child up out of the water to see us."[53] These images are not just poetic descriptions capturing Bond's vision of the world in the early eighties. They are powerful dramatic metaphors, drawn from the four motifs of sun, sea, rocks and land, used to demonstrate ways in which society, although superficially calm and peaceful, remains full of dangers that need radical surgery. In Bond's notebooks for the play, he comments: "It is not a play about the sea. It's about the room and the two islands. The two islands suggest eyes in a face."[54] This idea is successfully captured on the poster and program.

The program contains five poems and a story. They act as both a commentary on and a clarification of the play's themes.[55] "Always She Meant Well," the final poem, is subtitled "How a character is formed." The poem deals with Xenia and attempts to provide a rationale for her actions. In essence, the poem discusses Bond's premise that kindness, under our present circumstances, is wasted and instead of being perceived as such could be interpreted as hatred. Xenia does act graciously to Marthe; her concern over Marthe's illness, along with the gift of the waiter's crumb brush, are two examples. However, according to Bond, "Kindness became just another act of aggression," and Bond's intention is to show that Xenia's actions were misguided in a situation where kindness could not operate.[56] A critic suggested this was a side of Xenia incompatible with her actual characterization in Bond's production: "Anna Massey plays Xenia with a jarring harshness that seems to imply that such class enemies must become unpleasant."[57] Another commented, "Miss Massey responds with a steely haughtiness."[58] Massey also thought the presentation of Xenia was too narrow, focussing purely on her "bad" side. These criticisms lead us, quite naturally, to the subject of the acting in the production.

Daniel Baron Cohen, Bond's assistant, felt that the National's production of *Summer* should have been "the perfect laboratory for acting."[59] In practice, however, the production was fraught with difficulties. Peter Hall, then director of the National Theatre, recalls it as ". . . not being a happy time. . . [*Summer*] did not have the euphoric energy of *The Woman*."[60] The most significant complication in rehearsals at the National was the stylistic difference between Anna Massey's approach toward Xenia and that of Bond. From the beginning of rehearsals, Bond made a distinction between the way Xenia appears and the truth that lies behind her character:

> Xenia is always giving gifts, always smiling-killing people. . . She kept going around being good, being Lady Bountiful, but nobody was truly grateful. So she became frustrated, she became nervous and finally destructive, if you like, because she is a good woman. She was in the wrong situation.[61]

Philip Roberts, a commentator on Bond's work, has also described Xenia as a victim of her class:

> It is a classic Bond technique to say we have to change the world to stop people like Xenia having power. But also to say she is very pitiable in many ways. Xenia was brought up in a particular kind of class and the language she uses argues her own humanity and compassion.[62]

Bond does not say that Xenia is wicked:

> I do not want to show Xenia as evil—like some political fanatic who wants to label his enemies all the time. When Nazi concentration camp guards read their Christmas cards were they good?. . . We need to explore the various stages of deadness—and how she disguises it from herself.[63]

His concern is not with showing Xenia to be a "real" woman, but in exposing her *social* guilt, showing how she represents a certain "class" and, as such, cannot help but reinforce the very image she so desperately wants to be rid of.

Anna Massey's approach to the characterization of Xenia concentrated on producing a "human" element. Massey observes:

> Xenia is a very interesting character, obviously representative of the right wing. In Bond's terms, and in mine, a bad person. But in writing her character he wrote a very much more complex person than he allowed me to play. If you *just* have the wicked witch you are writing for children—if you have the good Marthe and the bad Xenia, it is very black and white, you don't have interesting interaction. If you allow Xenia to have something worthwhile to say; that is, she is not absolutely bad, you must allow her to say them. Bond has included good things in her character because he is a good playwright as well as a strong Marxist. He wrote things which were much more interesting in her character than he allowed me to play.[64]

In an interview with *Plays and Players*, Massey suggests that it was only as a result of Bond's direction that she emphasized the depravity of Xenia:

> [Bond has] written a very powerful argument for each side and the language was characteristically rich, but he couldn't bear to let my side score any points.[65]

The actress wanted to appear as Xenia, carrying all her emotional baggage. Massey suggests that it was Bond's unwillingness to allow her to adopt this approach which led to much of the conflict in rehearsals. She provides one example of a particular device she used as an actor:

> For the rehearsal period, you start to say "me" rather than "she." But it was very difficult to assume that. Bond didn't understand. So when you said "me," it was a direct confrontation with him.[66]

In response to the criticism that he only wanted Xenia to appear as evil, Bond observes:

> I am used to being accused of believing in concepts and encouraging practices I spend my creative life arguing against. . . I hope the text of *Summer* is itself proof that I would not connive at such crudity. Nor do I believe in "evil." Evil is yet another excuse—this time for our confusion and stupidity. It lets us off the hook. Evil may be forgotten but stupidity has to be paid for by all of us. Xenia is much more interesting than merely being evil.[67]

Bond also insists that there are no arguments that might excuse Xenia's actions: "In fact I do not know of any powerful arguments in favour of massacring women and children, and there are none to be found in the play."[68] Bond clarifies the situation:

> [Anna Massey] wished to show, at the end, that Xenia had a "good soul" and that in some way that redeemed her. And to be fair, the way we usually teach acting encourages this false view—it is after all the way many people see life. Well Hitler liked dogs but if at the end he had left his money to Battersea Dogs Home the ashes of Auschwitz would not be diminished by one grain and he would not have been redeemed. . . The play's point is that the argument of the "good soul" is a spurious convenience.[69]

Instead of Massey approaching the role "naturalistically," Bond wanted an actor in the observation of her role, showing its social function and "graphic sense," within the whole of society. In rehearsals for this production it became clear that Bond wanted to extract a certain style from Massey. Bond comments further on this approach:

> When I asked the actress who created the part of Xenia [Massey] to act this [final] scene as if she (not the others) were in a farce she said it would destroy the "beautiful" scene;" she wanted to play it with tragedy and sympathy. This I thought was a terrible insult to the dead at Auschwitz (Yes, I think art does matter . . .) because she was trying to capture a false nobility for herself—trying to appear to the audience as the girl in white on the balcony appeared to the German. Art can easily corrupt.[70]

Bond and Massey's views on a practical approach to Xenia were incompatible. The result, according to Bond, the critics and Massey, although for differing reasons, was a lopsided playing of the character.

The distinction between an emotional form of theatre and Bond's approach is understood by David Ryall who played Hemmel in the National Theatre's production:

> It's not possible to be unemotional because the characters are human beings; but you can have control over them so that you are not using them in the wrong way.[71]

This may be theoretically possible, but to what extent can this understanding effect a character and the way it is performed? Ryall states:

> The German puts this woman [Xenia] who has, unbeknownst to her, on one level been a kind of symbol for all the German is doing and what he is saying is that you must take responsibility for your life. For the things that are happening to you. The way you are being used. . . She does not know what her effect is and as a result is dangerous. She does know that, afterwards, her class or people have destroyed something of that country. Bond presents her with incontrovertible facts. He puts her on this island and gets this German to come and talk with her and he comes babbling out with all this stuff. Yet she does not run away. She is held there listening to something that is true and yet revolts her totally at the same time. We often said in rehearsals, "Why doesn't she get up and leave?"[72]

Confronted by another individual's perception of the truth, Xenia both dislikes and is mesmerized by what she hears.

Clearly, as a director, Bond needs a non-naturalistic approach to acting; a model that explores a character's social and political make-up. As expressed in Bond's poem, "To The Audience," an audience must use its own standards to judge the actions of characters. The cost of doing so is the exposure of its own values. Bond requires actors to be engaged in the process of uncovering characters' actions, so that an audience will not be seduced by the actor in the guise of the character, but able to understand their political motivations. First and foremost, Bond believes, this demystification is an actor's work:

> You are not there simply to get your "rocks off" or to have a good time. You are there to perform a certain job and the audience have to sense what that job is. You are not going in for some fake profundity, but you have thought about what you are doing.[73]

Stanislavsky was also interested in all the elements that created theatrical truth for an actor. The distinction between Stanislavsky and Bond is that Bond is not concerned with the manufacture of a stage reality. Bond requires an actor to understand and communicate the character's social and economic position. An actor approaching his work with a socio-economic per-

spective, will enable the audience to assess the character's political function. Bond's restlessness with theatrical reality is contained in an interview:

> I sometimes feel cheated when I see an old woman on stage portraying
> an old woman. Well yes, I think to myself, I know you can do that. I
> want to know something else, I want to know something more. And at
> that moment I can only do that by working directly with actors. I
> haven't formulated that very clearly into a set of exercises or state-
> ments. I really can only state the problem. Take scene five from *Sum-
> mer*, how are you going to act that? You don't want these people dig-
> ging down into their psyche and getting more nervous and tense. You
> need something else. Imagine someone swimming in the sea and think-
> ing they are drowning. What normally happens is that you get all these
> frantic gestures and that is what you get on stage. But the drowning
> man has his eye on the horizon. He sees where he has got to go. It's
> that eye on the horizon that really interests me.[74]

Marthe's death in performance is a moment worth considering, because it exemplifies the detachment required of the actor
playing Marthe and, at the same time, the emotion required of
the actor playing David to make it function as a truthful
moment of theatre. John Caulfield, the stage manager from the
National's production of *Summer*, describes a view of the production which may be representative of the more general
reaction:

> It is very sad at the end when Marthe dies and, because you have got to
> know her during the play, there is very little emotion attached to it.
> The audience is moved by the fact that somebody has died. This was
> not the case with *Summer*.[75]

In production, Bond was pleased Marthe's death did not bring
about a pre-conceived response from the audience; his notion
of theatre is violently opposed to producing "easy" solutions.
    Marthe's death also anticipates Bond's conscious use of TEs
in *The War Plays* and *Jackets*. A member of the audience
describes the event:

> In the preview of *Summer* which I saw [1/28/82] David lifted Marthe
> when she had died in the same way he lifted Ann after they had made
> love, very effectively linking life, sex, death and the possibility of new
> life as part of the same process.[76]

In rehearsals for *Summer*, Bond emphasized two major requirements for actors: concentration on the play's issues and discipline.

Bond maintained that audiences do not listen to an actor's voice, but rather to the workings of the mind. Consequently, he believes actors need to understand their character and pass on this interpretation to an audience:

> Another important thing is the head. . . It is quite extraordinary that actors can go through long speeches without thinking once . . . they do it by treating words as a form of music, or a form of sounds. They do not actually think. In my plays that is absolutely disastrous.[77]

Bond does not require actors to be relaxed during performance instead he wants the "alertness of the athlete and surgeon."[78] In the performances of *Summer* which I attended, most of the actors, especially Yvonne Bryceland, had an energy and focus appropriate to their characters' intentions. But how did Bond as a director make use of the theatre to convey his message?

Bond's characteristic demand in the National Theatre's production was for simplicity in scenic design. Both the set and lighting of *Summer* reflected the play's starkness. Hayden Griffin's set was dominated by a wall at the rear of the stage covered with imitation stone slabs. This revolved for the scene on the island becoming the execution wall. Significantly, the reverse side was also covered with slabs of rock. Throughout the play, the action took place on a set dominated by stone. Pete Mathers, in an analysis of the production, includes a detailed description of the setting:

> The high vertical walls were each interrupted, one by a door, the other by an opening. The back wall was topped by a steeply-pitched tiled roof. The roof was red, the tiled walls sand-coloured, the door green. . . Stage left, at the back, hung a cloth which evoked the Mediterranean sea and sky. The sea was a solid, linear blue, defining a straight horizon; the sky, spattered blue spots decreasing in density towards the horizon.[79]

The set provided a functional metaphor for the play itself: a warm mixture of bright colors, reminiscent of a European villa, able to transform itself into a harsher setting for the island.

According to Griffin, the change, from porch to beach, was originally conceived as occurring during the intermission:

> We designed this thrust stage, like a veranda, which flipped. On the other side was a rock face which became the island. The unfortunate thing was he [Bond] changed the position of the interval. Originally, the island was to be after the break, then Bond changed his mind. This came very late. Suddenly an act change became a scene change. This thing that had been manhandled into position had to be mechanically operated.[80]

Bond's interval change not only affected the setting but, according to Caulfield, shifted the play's emphasis by having a first half that ran ninety minutes and a second half of only fifteen. As a result, much of the audience left at the intermission believing it to be the end of the play.[81]

The "stylization" evident in Griffin's set design was emphasized by Bond's use of lighting:

> In my production of Summer, there were no blackouts in between the scenes. In fact, I like the lights to come up and the actors to become actors and walk off and then come on for their next scene as actors. I think the critics find that disconcerting. Someone dies on stage and then gets up and walks off. That seems to be saying something very beautiful and important about human beings. We can demonstrate to you the fact that other people die and suffer and then I, the actor, can get up and walk off the stage.[82]

Bond believes this technique is representative of his theatrical approach. However, some critics commented negatively on Bond's style: "Bond also managed to wreck one of the play's few moving moments by having the dead Marthe rise from her incumbent position to make an ungainly exit."[83]

In German program notes for a 1990 production of Summer, Bond expressed surprise that it stated that "'in spite' of the recent changes in Europe the play was still valid because it dealt with the 'eternal' questions of life and earth."[84] Bond's opinion is that Summer is a play which becomes more relevant with the end of the Cold War and re-ordering of the European social structure. In a letter Bond states:

> The changes do not alter the past—and the reappearance of Nazism and racism (did they ever go away?) in Europe are warnings.[85]

The changes to Europe's social fabric in 1990 caused Bond to emphasize the continued importance of *Summer*:

> I consider that the recent changes in Europe make very little difference to *Summer*. What Marthe says about Xenia and her world remains true. The bourgeois standards by which Xenia lived were corrupting in the way the German makes clear. Changes in Europe do not bring the ashes of Auschwitz back to human life. Xenia was able to corrupt notions such as kindness and justice to serve her own (conscious or unconscious) ends and it doesnt matter to the dead victims of Nazidom whether their killers understood why they killed them: Marthe judges their deeds and not their intentions. Doing this has human dangers, but it is also necessary for humane reasons.[86]

Summer is a play of contrasts. Just as there is an opposition between light and dark running throughout this piece, there are distinctions between order and disorder—the calmness of Marthe compared to the turbulent world of Xenia; between life and death—Ann and David compared to Xenia and Marthe; between past and present—how Xenia's and Marthe's lives are connected to the past. Bond confirms this notion of contrasts:

> The final scene only lasts a minute and ten seconds. It is a very important scene because the people there have to live within contrasts. Not in a bad sense, but by finding moral definition and creative energy by living in those contrasts. Finding a sense of social responsibility knowing that they are their society and their society is them.[87]

Difficulties with some of the play's acting style, mixed reviews and Bond's own uncertain response to the production meant that he was to take his next play, *The War Plays*, to the Royal Shakespeare Company. In *The War Plays*, Bond was not to deal with contrasts in society. Instead, he confronted the threatening subject of nuclear war and this issue of accepting responsibility for our actions:

> It's not a question of getting rid of H-bombs. You've actually got to get rid of a society that can create them and eventually let them off. You've got to get to a new form of humanity, a new form of social organisation. My theatre is to do with that.[88]

Notes

1 Kenneth Hurren, *What's On In London* February 1982: 23 and Eva Figes, *Times Literary Supplement* 5 February 1982: 133.

2 David Ryall, personal interview, 2 November 1989.

3 Edward Bond, notebooks for *Summer* quoted in Philip Roberts, "Edward Bond's 'Summer' a voice from the working class." *Modern Drama* XXVI 2 (1983): 130 and *Bond on File* compiled by Philip Roberts, (London: Methuen, 1985) 72 & 73. Copies of Edward Bond's notebooks are housed at Doheny Library, University of Southern California.

4 Bond quoted in *Modern Drama* 130 and *Bond on File* 73.

5 Edward Bond *Summer* (London: Methuen, 1982) 51.

6 Bond *Summer* 27.

7 Bond quoted in Philip Roberts, "Edward Bond's 'Summer': a voice from the working class:" *Modern Drama* 137.

8 David L. Hirst, *Edward Bond* (London: Macmillan, 1985) 79.

9 Edward Bond, taped correspondence to John Lamb, January 1982.

10 Hirst 80.

11 Edward Bond, interview with Nick Philippou, undated.

12 Roberts *Modern Drama* 129.

13 Bond quoted in *Modern Drama* 129.

14 Bond *Summer* 49.

15 Bond *Modern Drama* 129 & 130.

16 Edward Bond, draft introduction to *The War Plays* 23.

17 Edward Bond, "'The Romans' and the Establishment's Figleaf," *Guardian* 3 November 1980: 12.

18 Bond *Summer* 1.

19 Bond *Summer* 5.

20 Edward Bond, letter to David Jansen, 3 October 1989.

21 Edward Bond, personal interview, 14 December 1989.

22 Bond *Summer* 6/7.

23 Bond quoted in *Modern Drama* 132.

24 Bond quoted in *Modern Drama* 132.

25 Bond *Summer* 31.

26 Bond *Summer* 33.

27 *Modern Drama* 133.

28 Bond quoted in *Modern Drama* 133.

29 Bond *Summer* 35.

30 Bond *Summer* 33.

31 Bond *Summer* 27.

32 Bond quoted in *Modern Drama* 132.

33 Bond *Summer* 25.

34 Edward Bond, letter to Vassillis Paparassiliou, 25 August 1990.

35 Bond *Summer* 49.

36 Bond quoted in *Modern Drama* 130.

37 Bond *Summer* 40.

38 Bond *Summer* 41.

39 Bond *Summer* 39.

40 Bond *Summer* 16.

41 Bond *Summer* 39.

42 Edward Bond, letter to Kim Dambaek, 4 January 1983, quoted in *Bond on File* 51.

43 Bond *Summer* 39.

44 Bond quoted in *Modern Drama* 137.

45 Edward Bond, letter to Kim Dambaek, 4 January 1983.

46 Max Stafford-Clark, personal interview, 9 April 1990.

47 Peter Hall, personal interview, 17 July 1990.

48 Peter Hall, personal interview, 17 July 1990.

49 Bond *Summer* 50.

50 Bond *Summer* 44.

51 Bond *Summer* 54.

52 Bond *Summer* 27.

53 Bond *Summer* 33.

54 Bond quoted in *Modern Drama* 128.

55 These poems are reprinted in *Bond Plays: Four* (London: Methuen, 1992) 406-11.

56 Bond *Plays:Four* 411.

57 Mark Amory, *Spectator* 6 February 1982: 28.

58 Michael Coveney, *Financial Times* 28 January 1982: 21.

59 Daniel Baron Cohen, personal interview, 17 July 1990.

60 Peter Hall, personal interview, 17 July 1990.

61 Edward Bond, interview with Nick Philippou, 16 November 1981.

62 Philip Roberts, personal interview, 13 December 1989.

63 Edward Bond, letter to David Jansen, 3 October 1989.

64 Anna Massey, telephone interview, 22 January 1990.

65 Anna Massey, "Across the Water," *Plays and Players*, July 1991: 12.

66 Anna Massey quoted in David Jansen, "Working from 'Up Here,'" diss., Royal Holloway and Bedford New College, England, May 1989. 11.

67 Edward Bond, letter to the Editor, *Plays and Players*, 4 August 1991.

68 Bond letter to Editor.

69 Bond letter to Editor.

70 Edward Bond, letter to Vassilis Paparassiliou.

71 David Ryall, personal interview, 2 November 1989.

72 David Ryall, personal interview, 2 November 1989.

73 Bond taped correspondence.

74 Edward Bond, interview with Nick Philippou, undated.

75 John Caulfield, personal interview, 15 January 1990.

76 Margaret Biddle, "Learning and Teaching for Change and The Plays of Edward Bond," diss. University of York, October 1985, 84.

77 Bond taped correspondence.

78 Bond taped correspondence.

79 Pete Mathers, "Edward Bond Directs 'Summer' at the Cottesloe, 1982." *New Theatre Quarterly* II 6 May 1986: 145.

80 Hayden Griffin, personal interview, 21 February 1990.

81 John Caulfield, personal interview, 15 January 1990.

82 Bond taped correspondence.

83 Milton Shulman, *Standard* 28 January 1982: 22. A similar criticism was levelled at *Jackets*. See Chapter Six.

84 Edward Bond letter to Vassilis Paparassiliou.

85 Bond letter to Vassilis Paparassiliou.

86 Bond letter to Vassilis Paparassiliou.

87 Bond taped correspondence.

88 Bond, interview with Nick Philippou, 16 November 1981.

Chapter Five

The War Plays

The Royal Shakespeare Company's production of *The War Plays* received mixed reviews and was a frustrating experience for many of the actors and designers involved. Prior to the production, one critic stated that, in his opinion, *Great Peace*, the final part of the trilogy, was "one of the most significant new plays for many years."[1] But for many, the RSC's creative process and productions were less than satisfying. For example, Mal Calwood, as a result of the RSC's production, referred to *The War Plays* as "two evenings of pretentious rubbish."[2]

Before considering the practical elements associated with the production, how Bond worked on the plays, what concepts of acting he developed and the "aggro-effects" that are so much part of *The War Plays*, I shall study the text of the trilogy from a critical perspective.

The plays were initially conceived as individual units, not a trilogy. *The Tin Can People*, "A Short Play" in three sections, was written first. It was performed by Bread and Circuses Theatre Company in Birmingham, England, on May 4, 1984. Nick Philippou, at that time a recent graduate from the University of Birmingham and a director of the theatre company, asked Bond to write a play for the group. Bond recalls:

> Someone approached me with a particular problem; they wanted a play for a group of actors and I wanted to write a play that dealt with the problem of nuclear war. It was a depressing problem at the time I wrote the play and I wrote it to find out what is in our present society that you can be in a world of ruins and you do not recognise our society.[3]

Philippou comments on Bond's writing of *The Tin Can People*:

> I told Bond how many people were in the company, and he wrote a play for this number. I got the play. Didn't understand it and once I did, thought, "So what" because that can be a very immediate response to Bond's work on the page. Bond's plays are like snow-covered crevices, you go up to them and think, "Well, fine, snow" and you disturb a pebble on the top, the whole thing falls away and you suddenly see this massive crevice beneath you.[4]

Philippou's production was organized for the community and aimed at presenting the play's issues to the widest audience possible. Bond was not involved in the production process. Philippou remembers the play's controversial effect:

> The response from the audience was, "Why are we doing a play like *The Tin Can People* in a community centre? Surely this is not the kind of play that should be going round community centres and schools?" It was not just from the audience, this response came from the people who booked the show.[5]

In writing the next play of the series, *Red Black and Ignorant*, as it was finally called, Bond wanted to relate the difficulties of living in a post-nuclear world to the "more practical problems people have in their day-to-day lives."[6] Written for *Thoughtcrimes*, a two week presentation of plays, films, exhibitions and debates on issues raised by George Orwell's *1984* at the Barbican in London, the play was first seen at the Pit as a fifty minute workshop production entitled "The Unknown Citizen" on January 19 and 25, 1984. Despite being advertised as a workshop, the play was produced under normal performance conditions although it received no press reviews. *Red Black and Ignorant* has nine short scenes comprising an introduction and an examination of learning, love, eating, selling, work, the army, "giving up the name of human" and death. Bond has observed about the scenes: "It was necessary I put them in this nuclear context so that I began it from the idea that there had been a nuclear explosion."[7] Rejecting Orwell's view of the world, Bond sees Orwell as a "bit of an idiot" who failed to match his well-meaning intentions with his writings.[8] Bond felt that he wanted to write a third and more "real" play. This was *Great Peace*:

> The necessity of writing *Great Peace* was to get away from any sense of unreality, to try and be a social realist about something which is incred-

ibly bizarre and unreal. So I wanted this play to be a meditation on the suffering of people who are brought up in war, the brutality they commit in order to wage, survive and win war.[9]

Red Black and Ignorant became the trilogy's first play and *The Tin Can People* was performed in the Pit as the second part of *The War Plays*. They were presented by the Royal Shakespeare Company on May 29, 1985 with *Great Peace* joining the repertoire a few months later on July 17, 1985. They are known, collectively, as *The War Plays* trilogy.

Red Black and Ignorant is centered around the life, growth in understanding and death of a character already burnt in the womb by radiation from a nuclear bomb. The play is built on this paradox; it begins with a man never born talking of the life he did not lead. This bears a similarity to one of Bond's earlier plays *After the Assassinations*.

> I am seventy years old
> This is my dead son
> He is not yet born
> I am an actor and what I shall tell you has not
>   yet happened
> But it is already true.[10]

A ghost from the past, coming to the present in order to tell us about the future is a familiar enough dramatic device. But a blackened monster who has never lived informing us of his future, is indeed an unusual creation although one which, I will suggest, fits Bond's political dialectic.

Red Black and Ignorant traces what Bond interprets as the distortions of a capitalist society and how capitalism results in barbaric inhumanity; education breeds fear and hatred, a husband and wife argue with each other in this desolate landscape of marriage, children are treated as marketable commodities, a man leaves a woman pinned under a concrete beam in order to acquire a job and the Monster's son, now a soldier, spares the life of an old man he must kill and instead murders his father. One of the reasons the play is so interesting is the *way* Bond delivers his political "message." Through his use of the Monster, Bond comments on the function of the artistic impulse. For Bond, "art *is* the act and skill of showing. . . not [in] the object described or depicted."[11] The significance of this statement in the play is that in the monster "victims are martyrs who give us the chance to live in ways denied them."[12] The character's insight about the way his society operates is, according to Bond, the understanding we need in order to live: "The dead may give us life through our fictional characters."[13]

Red Black and Ignorant serves as an examination of the various stages in a person's life which train him to respond violently. This conclusion is expressed by the never-born but twice-dead father at the end of the play:

> My son learned it was better to kill what he loved
> Than that one creature who is sick or lame or old
> or poor
> or a stranger should sit and stare at an empty world
> and find no reason why it should suffer.[14]

Bond suggests that in the play's world, and ours, it is easier to annihilate the individual most loved and respected rather than hurt those we do not know. In this apparent contradiction lies a familiar Bondian premise expressed through the final lines of Part One:

> What is the freedom you gave me?
> Two fists of ash
>
> *He throws the ash on the ground*
>
> Where is the freedom in that?[15]

The play suggests that a capitalist society prevents us from knowing ourselves, our feelings. "For all of us," says the Monster, "there is a time when we must know ourself."[16] Society divorces true feelings from outward actions and thus ensures that a son can kill his father without remorse. This idea bears an outer resemblance to Orwell's concept of "double-think." In *Red Black and Ignorant*, Bond acknowledges the connection in confronting the paradox—the apparent saving of life by continuing to build a nuclear arsenal. In the *Guardian* newspaper on January 16, 1984, Bond demonstrates how, in his opinion, such contradictions are at work in the way society is constructed. Bond takes justice as an example:

> Our system of justice is said to be fair. We have a jury system, but juries
> decide facts not the meaning of facts. When they give verdicts they are
> obeying the law, not creating it. Existing law protects property relations
> that are manifestly unjust. And so our system of justice protects
> injustice.[17]

This notion of contradictory assumptions is explored further in
Great Peace. But it is in *Red Black and Ignorant* that a view of the
world is established where violence is a natural phenomenon of
an unjust society.

The Monster is representative of Bond's analysis of society.
He comments on people who, to preserve freedom, condemn
him and millions of others to the perpetual imprisonment of
death. By his very "existence," the character lives a contradiction. He is both a symbol of freedom (in Bond's terms the
Monster speaks "rationally" about life) and despair; he has been
killed by the very force he now understands. The Monster of
Red Black and Ignorant may be also be interpreted as a character
that makes sense of the play within global terms. Bond
observes:

> The Monster argues that a society that invests and labours to make
> freedom possible, and gambles on having to do it, ought not to be
> called civilization. That would be the greatest double-think. It should be
> given its proper name: barbarism.[18]

Divided into three sections, *The Tin Can People* focuses on
demoralized inheritors of earth seventeen years after the explosion of nuclear bombs. These survivors have formed a peaceful
commune living off five warehouses of tinned food. Their quiet
existence is invaded by a stranger, the First Man, who initially is
welcomed but, as death takes a hold on the group, is accused of
having contaminated them. He is hunted down and stabbed.
The title of the play's first section, "Paradise in Hell," suggests
the bomb has, ironically, brought heaven to earth. In his commentary, Bond states:

> The Tin Can Society is the most advanced society possible in the capi-
> talist world. Nuclear war has brought the audience's consumer society
> to its highest state of perfection. The Tin Can valley is heaven on
> earth.[19]

This easy alternative is rejected by Bond as the panacea to the human situation. Instead it could be suggested that *The Tin Can People* shows the difficulty of creating a new society when certain basic truths are ignored. For example, the reality of their condition has removed the tin can people from a previously experienced human situation and placed them in an alien environment. However, their behavior remains consistent; they continue viewing the world as if unchanged by nuclear explosions. But they show their "humanness" when they confront their own mortality as human beings. In this situation attitudes quickly change from contentment to paranoia. Bond shows that whilst these people may live together in a paradise, it is a post-nuclear one and one built on insecure foundations. As the murder of the Gravedigger's Boy in *Lear* brings an abrupt conclusion to his pastoral, escapist world, the dream existence of the tin can people is shattered as death gradually destroys them. The group thinks they have created a place without the possibility of further harm. The tin can people live with uncertainty and danger of radiation, but believe the problem is contained. Bond has likened the arrival of the First Man to the coming of Satan:

> Anyone who appears in the Tin Can People's valley must come from outside heaven—and be Satan. . . They have been corrupted, as all who live in heaven must be.[20]

Much of the play's action occurs in the penultimate scene; the Fourth Woman pretends she is dead and rehearses how to imitate the stillness of death, the Second Woman tries to kill the First Man but is restrained by the First Woman, the Third Man also attacks him but then saves his life. It is an extraordinarily violent scene and necessarily so. But what remains important for Bond is that the *cause* of the suffering be clear:

> In an explosion each speck of dust points to the other specks and to the explosion—each event in the scene is about the other events. We can only understand history and chaos by reading the specks of dust, they are the only maps we have of history and chaos.[21]

The Tin Can People does not, as one critic has suggested, show "that we may have to suffer a nuclear holocaust to expose the injustices of our day."[22]

Great Peace is the final part of *The War Plays*. It was the final play to go into rehearsal and join the production at the Pit.[23] The play pivots on instructions issued in the first scene. Due to insufficient resources, all soldiers must destroy one infant from their street, "promptly and humanely."[24] The Mother from *Red Black and Ignorant* has a new child and, initially, *Great Peace* focuses on her soldier son's dilemma over whether to kill a neighbor's child or his own sibling. In a grotesque scene, reminiscent of the atrocities of *Saved*, the soldier returns the neighbor's baby unharmed and instead suffocates his Mother's child with the floorcloth. Like the Monster's murder in *Red Black and Ignorant*, and the Corporal's shooting of the Son in *Great Peace*, the killing is designed to awaken the audience to the extreme brutality of this world.

Great Peace focuses on many sensitive issues, one of which is a woman's love for her child. (This is developed further in *Jackets*). It is a feeling which the actress Maggie Steed, who first played the part of the Woman in *Great Peace*, initially under Bond's direction, described as "very human and very accessible."[25] However, if this is a sensitive issue, then a child's death is even more tender. It should be emphasized that Bond does not write about infanticide for gratuitous reasons but in order to make a political point. For these reasons the two deaths need to be examined alongside one another.

The murder of the Woman's baby is pointless, a human life sacrificed to comply with a military order. In scene eight, a soldier refuses to pick up a cigarette packet and is shot for his stubbornness. The two incidents are situated in this way not simply for dramatic effect but because they force a comparison. What we witness is the death of innocence, the baby at the mercy of authoritarian structures, and the slaying of a soldier, who has been exposed to and accepted, even if unconsciously, the organization of society. Despite these crucial differences, the horror and futility of both deaths is apparent and such juxtaposition allows Bond to demonstrate the similarity of these incidents. By his placement of these two moments, Bond attempts to demonstrate how the origin of aggressive behavior is founded in social circumstances.

At the heart of this play is a concept similar to that used in *Red Black and Ignorant*: the paradox of illusion.

> If we blame the Woman for the murder of the child she asks us why we drove her mad?. . . If the audience cannot understand this she would point to our bombs and say we were mad. She pretended a rag was a baby: we pretend bombs save our lives and we will kill untold millions on the say-so of rulers who own our culture and determine the norms of social sanity.[26]

The Woman treats the bundle of rags she carries as a child. This is an important image; the Woman's empty bundle accuses an audience of failing to reform their society and thus perpetuates her illusion. Clinging to the bundle of rags she still wants to believe is her child, the Woman continues to trudge through the wilderness. On this journey towards greater understanding of her world, the Woman needs the fake baby to guard against insanity. Both the Woman and the audience need "appropriate levels of illusion in order to observe the real world (without fantasy or illusion)."[27] So the Woman's torn sheet is similar in function to the theatre for an audience; both provide necessary illusions that give access to reality. In a letter, Bond clarifies this transformation of the Woman's baby into rags:

> Early in the play I let the bundle unravel into a sheet so that the audience are in no doubt about this; but so self-enclosed is the woman at this moment (or rather so wrapped up in the pain of the world) that she doesn't even notice that she's let the bundle unravel. . . When she is able to face certain questions without being driven mad by them. . . then she can abort the false baby. Until then the bundle is like a real bandage round a psychic wound.[28]

Illusion and reality are connected with one of the most significant and complex symbols in *Great Peace*. It occurs at the end of scene ten. A stage direction states: "*A moment later the baby raises a hand and gives one short cry that is lower than would be expected.*"[29] This gesture is made by the "real" child left in the Woman's care by its deceased mother. It juxtaposes "reality" with the delusions of the Woman—here is a "real" baby that makes a "real" gesture, unlike the Woman's illusion that she carries a child in her rags. So why does she desert the "real" child? It is an example of an occasion when the Woman confuses illusion and reality, connecting the two different worlds of artificial and "real" experience for an audience. The baby's gesture is only "real" in the theatre but its effect is felt in a wider social sphere. Like Brecht, Bond wants dramatic analysis in the theatre and needs an audience to "think above the action," not disregard emotional responses but "think feelings and feel thoughtfully."[30] The image of the child's hand functions in a similar way for both an audience and the Woman; both use illusion in order to observe the real word. At the end of *Great Peace*, the Woman recognizes that her baby is finally dead:

Empty
Nothin in it
I kept it in case it comes in 'andy
Rags are useful out 'ere or at your place
Empty nothin[31]

It has taken the entire play for her to appreciate this and, significantly, her understanding comes at the end of the trilogy. For many, the plays end on a bleak note; the death of the Woman in the wilderness. However, for Bond, this is not a negative vision:

She says to the younger people: I will not go back to your city—instead
I will walk into the wilderness and *in that way* will become one of the
foundations.[32]

The absence of names in *The War Plays* holds a significance for an audience and the danger, of providing characters with names or titles, is they are often "little better than prison numbers. . . Would war memorials be more useful if after each named dead there were the names of those he or she had killed?"[33] It is possible to see Bond's reluctance at using names to label characters as one key to understanding the dialectic of *The War Plays*. By not classifying those in the play, Bond suggests that he does not want to mold an audience into a particu-

lar view. He wants them to discover for themselves the individ-
uality which fills his characters.

Confusion about the uniqueness of a character's identity may
arise as a result of double casting, as it is possible to dou-
ble/triple cast the trilogy. This was a technique used in the
Royal Shakespeare Company production. To assist an audience
who viewed the entire play at one sitting, Bond carefully
orchestrated many of the characters' identities.[34] Directorial
decisions about casting needed to be made at an early stage
because Bond found it possible, by doubling or tripling the
parts an actor plays, to influence the tone of the production.
For example, the soldier son was the same in *Red Black and
Ignorant* and *Great Peace*. The Woman from *Great Peace* was the
Monster's mother, and Woman 1, from the same play, was the
much older First Woman from *Red Black and Ignorant*. Bond
maintained that in the RSC production, an actor should not
make any psychological connection between characters. However, he stressed that certain similarities could be drawn out in
performance by the same actor playing the role. Consequently,
an audience in witnessing these plays would understand how
both men and women in the play arrived at answers.

The trilogy does not contain "sentimental imagery," or tell
"how little we are to learn from such an experience."[35] Instead
The War Plays, admittedly in characteristically brutal fashion,
express Bond's hope that the fiction of his characters becomes
our reality; the theatrical experience evaporates, leaving behind
an audience who learn from the dead about how to prevent self-
extinction.

It is possible to interpret *The War Plays* differently.

> You can see them straight forwardly as a record of the consequences of
> nuclear wars. But also they can be seen psychologically—as patterns of
> the devastation within the psychology, which produces the violence of
> the lout and the yuppie, the posturing ignorance of the racist, the self-
> satisfied intolerance of the affluent. As a record of the devastation of
> the mind.[36]

Violence is at the heart of many of Bond's plays. This is a trend
not to be explored in depth here, but any overview of *The War
Plays* must include a discussion of this "shock" technique.

Walter Benjamin, the German Marxist critic, in his essay "The Work of Art in the Age of Mechanical Reproduction," argues that works of art have an "aura" of uniqueness, privilege, distance and permanence about them.[37] However, duplicating this originality on film ensures that the camera penetrates life and examines it closely. This shifts the peaceful contemplation of a picture into frightening clarity as we are able to stand up close and examine it. Benjamin, in this essay, discusses the "shock" value of film and how it creates "montage," "the connecting of dissimilar to shock an audience into insight."[38] Although, for the most part, Bond's work has not been exposed to celluloid, he is a writer who closely examines the details of life, as if through a camera lens, and produces immediate images similar to the effect described by Benjamin.[39] Accused of gratuitously shocking his audience, an accusation Bond has consistently denied, *The War Plays* in general, and *Red Black and Ignorant* in particular, often use such "shock tactics," sudden changes in direction which rock an audience from side to side in their emotional loyalties. Many other writers, such as Pirandello and Brecht, used this technique before Bond. What distinguishes Bond's use of the confrontational device is the extent and depth to which it is applied as a dramatic technique. For example in Part One of the trilogy, the Son retreats from murdering his neighbor, instead substituting his father. The Son's kindness in not killing the old man is a reversal of our expectations and, to unsettle an audience still further, is accompanied moments later by the murder of his own father. This action leaves an audience unsure of who can be believed or trusted. Such an approach of exploiting an audience's attitude occurs in many of Bond's plays. The scene from *Saved* where a child is stoned to death in a park is the most notable example, along with *Early Morning* with its cannibalism and lack of sexual discrimination, and *The Sea* where Hatch stabs the drowned body of Colin. Bond calls such a frictional approach to an audience's responses an "aggro-effect," an aggression effect. In an article published in the *Canadian Theatre Review*, Bond describes the need for a writer to disturb an audience through his work:

I've had to find ways of making that "aggro-effect" more complete, which is in a sense to surprise them, to say "Here's a baby in a pram—you don't expect these people to stone that baby. Yet—snap—they do."[40]

Margaret Biddle, who has written on Bond's plays, indicates that such expressions of violence do more than simply represent reality:

Clearly atrocities happen daily in our world but Bond's world does not deal in attempts at realism. We need another way of reading his theatre. . . The nature of his plays deal with the relationship between individuals and the society they live in. Society and the images come to embody aspects of his analysis of that relationship.[41]

In *The War Plays*, the function of "aggro-effects" is to force an audience into thinking about the causes of such actions. Bond discusses the function of the effect:

If you have the effrontery to say, "I am going to use an aggressive 'aggro-effect' against an audience," if you have the impertinence to say that—and I've just said it—then it must be because you feel you have something desperately important to tell them. If they were sitting in a house on fire, you would go up to them and shake them violently. . . And so it's only because I feel it is important to involve people in the realities of life that I sometimes use those effects.[42]

The startling images in *The War Plays* puts an audience in the position of having to witness horrors which, in Bond's terms, they may permit through their social complacency. For example, in an article published to coincide with the workshop production of *Red Black and Ignorant*, Bond describes how Dr. David Owen, then a leader of Britain's Liberal/Social Democratic Party Alliance might appear on television with a model of a child:

And suppose that, using his medical knowledge, he had demonstrated with the help of a blow-torch the effect of nuclear explosions on a child: the burning-out eyes, the hacking-off of the limbs, the opening of the stomach and the probing of the entrails with the blow-torch. As he did so, he could have explained that to protect the middle way he felt it necessary to risk ordering men and women, for a reasonable salary, to perform these atrocities on millions of children and older people.[43]

Besides being an attack on Owen, the article shows how a conscious use of provocative language and imagery confronts and startles. "Aggro-effects," as used in *The War Plays*, can be seen as both a way of shocking an audience and an extensive presentation of Bond's view about nuclear war. This idea of an "aggro-effect" connects with many images in Bond's plays. Two strains it can be argued, are dominant in this play: the use of the "violated sheet" and the murdered or abandoned child.

The "violated sheet" seems to represent for Bond the destruction of comfort and escapism which he wants to effect in the theatre. For example, the sheet occurs as a motif for the Gravedigger's Boy in *Lear*, where it is torn up during his murder; comparable are the material which is cut up by Hatch in *The Sea* and the sheet which drapes Brian's corpse in *Jackets II* and becomes a shroud for Mrs Lewis. The murdered or abandoned child has always been a hallmark of Bond's plays. Representing the future of society, it is consistent with Bond's view that in *Great Peace* babies are murdered rather than the elderly, who presumably represent the past. In *Saved, Narrow Road to the Deep North, The Bundle* and *Jackets I* the infant symbolizes the world as presently constituted. As such, the child is always destroyed.

During the genesis of *The War Plays*, Bond developed various theoretical models to explain the acting and directing style of the trilogy. These can also be applied to much of his later work. They include Bond's idea of a "gap" caused by the separation of story and character; "T" acting, designed to fill this "gap" meta-text, formed as a result of this division of story and character; and TEs.

In Bond's drama, a character is a complex individual, one who should not simply tell the story, but fill the "gap" where an audience may learn about itself. Bond states:

> A story cant be reduced to characterisations—that the story exists as it is because the characters are what they are, is wrong. The gap has to be filled with philosophy.[44]

It is vital that the action of a play be more than just the creation of character; it should contain individuals who act as springboards for an audience's ideas. In a letter, Bond comments: "a stage is as specific to an audience, as a dock is to a court of law. The performance is always out of the character's hands."[45] For

Bond, it is always an audience that must judge, using the stage space to observe life is meaningless. As this extract shows, Bond's theatre is analytical:

> It's as if there were a bag full of groceries. These are the character. The stage must spill the contents of the bag. How they are picked up is in fact the performance. So the stage insists on social observation and not merely reproduction.[46]

An audience should not just be presented with what they can see in life, but challenged in ways that are uniquely characteristic of Bond's philosophy.

If Bond's theatre is used to inject philosophy into our lives, then it puts Bond's concept of "T" acting at opposite ends of the scale to Strasberg's "method" approach. "Method acting," Bond maintains, "has degenerated into the 'treatment.'"[47] Bond is against the notion of making his plays function in that way and any form of psychological acting which, in his opinion, reduces theatre to a crude trivialization of life. An action carried out on stage must take longer than the same incident carried out in "real" life. This brings Bond to the conclusion, "a person does, an actor shows" and so an actor moves from attempting to "become" the character and enters a realm of demonstrating the social context because he now "shows" us his character.[48] In acting *The War Plays*, or any play by Edward Bond, an actor needs to separate the psychological from the philosophical. It may be possible to build up a whole directorial interpretation on this psychological basis. However in order to accomplish a philosophical view, a director must *interpret* the play. This interpretation demands a new form of acting: "T" acting. As Bond states, the entire theatrical experience is one built on illusion and is essentially unnatural:

> An actor cannot be the character he acts (obviously). There is always a gap—and this gap gives rise to the question: why is the actor acting —why do we have plays—why do we go to the theatre. The gap demands a philosophy and not merely an aesthetics. If we aesthetisize food, we turn a natural act into a cultural act. We must eat. But theatre isnt a natural act in the same way. . . why does the actor pretend and why do we suspend belief—and cannot always do so even if we want to?[49]

A concrete example of the practicalities of "T" acting can be taken from Bond's account of his direction of *The War Plays*:

> In *Red Black and Ignorant* the Mother dresses her son and sends him out to kill. When he was a boy she dressed him and sent him out to school or an errand. Should we show the woman's contradictions by subtly suggesting that she dresses the soldier as she dressed the boy, handling his helmet as if it was his schoolcap and so on? After trying a number of things we did this: as the mother put the soldier into his jacket she dropped it. He stood awkwardly at attention and she bowed low before him to pick it up. The movements were slightly metaphorized. The woman who was in control of the kitchen was shown in all her social weakness. The soldier was shown as a child.[50]

Bond's concept of a "gap," between the story and its characters, means that not only is an alternative approach to acting needed, but that a metatext is created. This is a phrase used mainly in connection with Bond's play *September*, produced in Canterbury Cathedral in 1989, but it should be discussed here because of its relevance to *The War Plays*.

By metatext, Bond has conceived a style which ensures that actors do not theorize, but rather analyze on stage. This analysis occurs through the metatext, the abolition of a sub-text. In notes for the actors of *September*, he comments on this idea:

> If we begin from the *meta*-text we can stage the audience's reality— obliging them to choose; if we create a *sub*-text we substitute interpretation of the audience and make them prisoners of their reality.[51]

At a conference for the National Association for the Teaching of Drama in October, 1989, Bond provided a further definition of a metatext:

> *We* need a metatext . . . a text on top which will create situations in the drama which will then produce various forms of human beings and we can then say, right, well that's fine, we can see how that human being produced him or herself in that situation. That I believe to be what actually happens in society.[52]

In his definition of a metatext, it can be seen that Bond dislikes any secrecy or mysteriousness connected with a play. This, he believes, is the trap of playing a sub-text; it comes across as being "profound interpretation," but is really only a shallow view of reality.[53] Such freedom is a further characteristic of the metatext abolishing an actor's need to interpret the play's hidden meaning:

> It means that the actor isnt required (as in some political theatre) to put a unifying objectivity between himself and the character: the metatext to be played with the same involvement and the same intention as the text and sub-text: the metatext becomes the objective, analytical view—and it is the involvement in both the play and the character: in playing the metatext the player is the character.[54]

What Bond wants to do with TEs is demystify the "reality" that occurs on stage in order to create rationally. As he states; "Nothing really happens [on stage] because this is a play" which connects with the earlier idea of artificiality.[55] The function of TEs in the trilogy can best be summed up in one of Bond's letters:

> [TEs] illuminate the moment of a passage so that the spectators learn the constituents of their lives—that they are not merely readers of what their hand writes (as if it came with the otherness of a form or a poster) but that they choose their acts. These acts must be put into real contexts so that decisions are made and lived with or died for.[56]

In *The War Plays*, Bond constructs a dramatic pattern where the meaning of each play is no longer contained within the story but resides in its analysis. In practical terms, Nick Philippou, a director of Bond's work, explains the purpose of TEs:

> It's not a question of an audience being clever. It's a question of understanding why a play is like it is. I don't think a spectator would know that in order to get that effect Picasso has used a blue wash. Certainly I do not expect an audience member to go out and say, "That was connected with that." But our experience is enriched by our knowledge of image connections whether we are an educated member of the audience or not.[57]

Bond insists that emotions simply for their own sake makes emotions passive, standing between concepts and feeling.[58] According to Bond, what must happen in the theatre is that ideas about society must be challenged, and this will cause a consequent shift in emotions. So it is vital for the actor to draw distinctions between "reality" and the stage, which may use familiar incidents but should not attempt to replicate them.

The Tin Can People was already written when the Royal Shakespeare Company asked Bond for a new play on nuclear war. So he wrote two other works, *Red Black and Ignorant*, then *Great Peace*, and included *The Tin Can People* within the overall structure. Nick Hamm was appointed by the RSC as a "staff director" primarily to assist Bond in the administrative side of running the trilogy. There is little evidence to suggest co-directing alone damaged the production. On the contrary, one critic suggested that the acting of the plays adopted a "Brechtian" approach—"hard edged, vivid, intelligent, dispassionate and heartfelt at one and the same time."[59] This is what Bond attempted to extract from the cast whilst he worked with them producing, what was called, by one critic at least, "an ensemble miracle."[60] However, Bond left rehearsals after the opening of *The Tin Can People* at the end of May 1985 explaining that he was not getting useful work from the actors:

> I was disturbed by the nature of the work we were doing and dissatisfied with the results. I felt that if I were not there, they would at least be able to cobble together an RSC production. I felt I was denying the actors their habitual tricks and devices but, at least within those working conditions, I was unable to produce in them the degree of precision, intensity and observation that I wanted. Invariably they wanted to act the peripheral and not its essential structures.[61]

According to Ian McDiarmid, who played the Monster in *Red Black and Ignorant*, the First Man in *The Tin Can People*, the Officer and Middle Aged Man in *Great Peace*, rehearsals were "an unhappy time for everybody involved."[62] Various theories have arisen to explain difficulties experienced by the Company: having Bond as director, the clash between his acting theories and practice, and the problems of Bond working within a structure such as the RSC. Despite difficulties during rehearsals, some interesting performance concepts arose:

> In *The War Plays*, I wrote a scene where I said the woman kisses the man with infinite politeness and I think that's perhaps the best way of doing it. But in rehearsal the actress grabbed the hand, almost bit it off and threw it away like a bit of waste paper and it was absolutely right. It was the opposite to what I'd written. If she'd ignored the hand and said—"I'm not into a hand kissing scene at the moment," I'd have said—"Well the script is there and you bloody well do it." In other words, you can't have total license. You've got to follow the script. The

script is there to create certain problems, but her situation was absolutely fine. I think that if she'd have played it longer she would have
found some other way of doing it.[63]

This is an indication of Bond's flexibility as a director. If an
actor provides an honest response, Bond is willing to see the
importance of overriding his text and any preconceived notions
he holds as to the way a moment should be presented. Such an
incident demonstrates one of the advantages of having the
writer as director.

The major difficulty for Bond in rehearsing *The War Plays*
was the nature of the company's acting. As Bond has commented: "In the end I was not afraid they [the ensemble] would
lecture the audience with ideas—but they would lecture them
with emotions: would tell the audience how to feel."[64] Bond
was attempting a different approach to acting antithetical to an
emotional approach taken by many RSC actors. In an interview,
Bond describes the difficulty of trying to create in this way:

> I wanted to talk about theatre in a different way and it just wasn't
> on. . . The actors were desperate for jobs, security and all the rest of it
> and they were saying—yes, we would like to look at things differently or
> whatever, but it wasn't true and I think that they got afraid.[65]

Initially, rehearsals of the play, conducted in Bond's tradition
of intricate textual analysis, generated a great deal of emotion.
Indeed, Bond is of the opinion that this process should be challenging for actors: "how else can we can comfort ourselves at
the pain our characters suffer."[66]

In London, the RSC has two permanent repertory theatres
running different productions simultaneously. Consequently,
with few of the trilogy's actors coming from outside the RSC,
this meant that most of the cast had other production commit-
ments. One characteristic of Bond's work in performance is the
amount of time needed for rehearsal. But with an already full
workload, some actors felt uneasy by the demands that were
being placed on them. David Shaw-Parker, composer of the
music for the trilogy and an observer at many of the plays'
rehearsals, has observed that Bond's frustration with professional theatre may have contributed to the production
difficulties:

Its rather like working in the BBC; the RSC imposes certain restrictions, I mean even things like overtime. When you are working on something that means that much to you and, at the end of the day, if somebody says you cannot have the guy on the electrics until 11:30 pm, and you passionately want to start at 8pm, those are frustrations that can build up.[67]

Steed comments that another difficulty of *The War Plays* in production lay in the trilogy's organization at the Pit:

Bond was treated badly at the RSC. If people are going to come to an occasion like *The War Plays* then an audience have to be cared for and looked after. It is difficult material talking about our greatest fears and . . . you should know that an audience may have this extraordinary experience.[68]

As an audience member, I certainly never had a sense of being "cared for" during the RSC's production of *The War Plays*. Staged in a small theatre never conceived for use as a performance space, the Pit is situated in the most inaccessible part of the Barbican complex. Despite the length of *The War Plays*, the RSC made no concessions over performance times which meant when the evening finished—at around 11:45 pm—we had to find our way out of a deserted building only to discover that the London transport system was closing and that getting home would be difficult. This insensitivity on the RSC's part undoubtedly contributed to the trilogy's lack of popularity.

Bond believes that the pressures of contemporary British theatre establishments were also an important factor in the production's critical failure. To justify this accusation, Bond cites an amateur production of *The War Plays* in Manchester:

What I found with the people in Manchester was that they needed the play to try and understand their lives, to try and make it useful for them in that way, and this went a long way to making the play work. I think they lacked some of the skills that you'd find in a more professional production. They lacked an ability to relate very, very closely to a lot of the language, the nuances if you like. . . I found it a truthful performance. . .[69]

Whatever the causes of Bond's instability to work on the RSC's production of *The War Plays*, the result failed to accurately represent his work in performance.

Red Black and Ignorant, in both the 1984 and 1985 productions, was acted on a bare stage with minimal use of props and no scenery. The concrete beam which collapses in scene six was represented by a wooden bench. This bench also provided actors with a place to sit and serve meals, represented by a loaf of bread the Monster's wife cut into slices. The most striking visual effect of the production was the Monster. Totally black, his skin, hair and clothes singed, the Monster appeared, as noted in the text, "as if carved from a piece of coal."[70] In a similar way, *The Tin Can People* used little scenery although a mound had been constructed upstage right, enabling the community to be isolated initially from the First Man. Empty tin cans were strewn across the space and, as if to emphasize the ragged nature of the group, the costumes of these holocaust survivors appeared torn and in shreds. Despite this, many of them seem to have made attempts to shield themselves from the harsh effects of a nuclear winter.

Like the other two plays, *Great Peace* was also performed on a bare stage with all activities between Mrs Symmons and Mother 1, for example, being isolated by separate pools of light using a minimum of props. Stewart Laing, who designed the plays, commented on the props' specificity:

> The nature of the tin cans, for example, whether they should be army supply. We did some research and discovered soldiers eat from exactly the same tins as everyone else. We had endless discussions on the tin cans; whether the cans in *The Tin Can People* should be different from the tin cans of *Great Peace*. The same goes for the bread. Bond was absolutely meticulous.[71]

The concept of minimalism is important to Bond as director:

> Everything on the stage is a gun and the moment a gun appears on stage it has a particular potency, a particular charisma, because people can save lives or they can die with a gun.[72]

With the RSC production, only the most essential lighting, set design and costumes were used. These elements were retained after Bond left the rehearsal process. Laing observed:

There was very little set. Just background to show off the different elements of the play. . . The first play [*Red Black and Ignorant*] was very
small scale. Edward kept saying "agitprop." The second play [*The Tin
Can People*] was more expansive and *Great Peace* was a large expanse.
Edward did a diagram, circles and squares, to explain the scale. I was
not used to such detailed analysis.[73]

Another element of the production, uncomplicated in its
approach, was the program. This was simply a folded sheet containing Bond's poem *Silence*.[74] The poem was copied onto a
picture of the Cenotaph in London. The Cenotaph is a com-
memoration of war dead buried abroad and thus can be seen as
a glorification of the sacrifices of war. *Silence* discussed the
paradox of remembering dead from warfare whilst, at the same
time, perpetuating an unfair society which, in Bond's view,
must destroy itself if it continues in its present form.

Far from showing "cozy scenes of cooperation" and "falsely
redemptive endings," *The War Plays* continue Bond's investiga-
tion of complex human situations. The plays never compromise
Bond's vision that changes in society will only come about as a
result of understanding.

I think that in order to change society then there is suffering. I don't
like the idea that there *must* be because that is almost a religious attitude—in other words suffering is good for you and you will achieve
through suffering. The suffering is incidental it is imposed by the
forces of stupidity which resist change.[75]

As a director of *The War Plays*, Bond played a critical role in
the transition of his text from page to stage. His presence at
rehearsals allows actors to guide and shape their parts and getting involved in rehearsals enables Bond to remind actors of
their wider social role. In notes to the cast of *September*, Bond
indicates the importance of acting:

A play cant make all its audience "better people." It is its moral duty to
make some of them worse. That's a responsibility actors shouldnt take
lightly. If you do your work well some of the audience will leave the
theatre better people and some worse. It is my devout wish![76]

Bond's drama uses theatre as a social space, one which forces
people to define their identity. Leading them into a post-

nuclear world, he hopes that an understanding of the situation, reached in the context of the play's fictionalized narrative, will penetrate the lives of those witnessing it. A complicated web of awkward production difficulties surrounded the RSC's performances of *The War Plays*.[77] Having seen the trilogy, I would suggest that whilst Bond may have made advances in acting theories, the performance conditions at the RSC obscured their practical implementation. Certainly the performance I witnessed of *The War Plays* (*Pièces de Guerre*) at the Avignon Festival in 1994, directed by Alain Françon, proved to those who saw the plays that, beyond any doubt, the trilogy is among the most remarkable cycles written by a contemporary British playwright. Staged in the open-air Court of St Joseph, the performances began at 10pm and lasted to 5am—all three plays being presented in the same evening.

With the Lancaster production of his next play, *Jackets*, Bond returned to a university setting where he attempted to startle his audience into further social realization.

Notes

1   Malcolm Hay, "Edward Bond British Secret Playwright" *Plays and Players* (June 1985): 9.

2   Mal Calwood, "Whistling in the Wilderness" *Red Letters* 19 (1985): 11.

3   Edward Bond, personal interview, 14 December 1989.

4   Nick Philippou, personal interview, 15 December 1989.

5   Nick Philippou, personal interview, 4 October 1990.

6   Edward Bond, personal interview, 14 December 1989.

7   Edward Bond, personal interview, 14 December 1989.

8   Edward Bond, personal interview, 14 December 1989.

9   Edward Bond, personal interview, 14 December 1989.

10   Edward Bond, *Choruses from "After the Assassinations"* (London: Methuen, 1983) 31.

11   Edward Bond, draft introduction to *The War Plays* 13.

12   Bond introduction 32.

13   Bond introduction 32.

14   Edward Bond, *The War Plays* (London: Methuen, 1991) 38.

15   Bond *War* 39/40.

16   Bond *War* 38.

17   Edward Bond *Guardian* 16 January 1984: 9.

18   Bond *Guardian*.

19   Bond *War* 345.

20   Bond introduction 23.

21   Bond *War* 348.

22   Robert D. Hostetter, "Drama of the Nuclear Age," *Performing Arts Journal* 11 1988: 94.

23 In his "Commentary" on *The War Plays*, Bond suggests a way of revising his original scheme, placing the first eight scenes of *Great Peace* before *The Tin Can People*. This approach was not used by the Royal Shakespeare Company in the 1985 production but was adopted by Alain Françon for the Centre Dramatique National de Savoie production of *The War Plays* (*Pièces de Guerre*) at the Avignon Festival 1994, and, subsequently, on tour.

24 Bond *War* 102.

25 Maggie Steed, personal interview, 9 October 1990.

26 Bond introduction 41.

27 Bond *War* 355.

28 Edward Bond, letter to Hilde Klein Hagen, 12 September 1987.

29 Bond *War* 162.

30 Bertolt Brecht quoted in Terry Eagleton, *Marxism and Literary Criticism* (London: Methuen, 1976) 67.

31 Bond *War* 238.

32 Edward Bond, letter to Roberta Pazardjiklian, 5 January 1990.

33 Bond introduction 43.

34 Occasionally the three plays were shown on the same day.

35 Paul M. Frazier, "Science Fiction Drama" diss., Michigan State University 1988, 66/7.

36 Edward Bond, letter to K. Oakley, 21 April 1990.

37 Reprinted in Walter Benjamin's *Illuminations* (London: 1970.)

38 Terry Eagleton, *Marxism and Literary Criticism* (London: Methuen, 1976.) 63.

39 Bond contributed to the screenplay of Antonioni's 1966 film *Blow-Up* also *Michael Kolhaas, Laughter in the Dark, Walkabout* and *Nicholas and Alexandra*. In a letter to Richard Scharine, quoted in Scharine, *The Plays of Edward Bond*, (Lewisburg: Bucknell University Press, 1976 159) Bond states: "Don't waste reader's time by making them read about this nonsense. . . You can't honestly pick out my contributions to the films, they are so adulterated." During 1990/1 Edward Bond wrote a trilogy of short television plays, *Olly's Prison*, commissioned by the BBC. These plays were filmed in London between December 1991/January 1992. Bond has also written a film script of Melville's *Moby Dick*. At the time of writing *Moby Dick* has not been filmed and the script is unpublished.

40 Edward Bond and Christopher Innes, "Edward Bond; from Rationalism to Rhapsody", *Canadian Theatre Review* No. 23 (Summer 1979): 109 and 111.

41 Margaret Biddle, "Learning and Teaching for Change and The Plays of Edward Bond," diss., University of York, October 1985, 10/11.

42 Bond and Innes 113.

43 Bond *Guardian.*

44 Edward Bond, letter to Patricia Bond, 15 March 1989.

45 Edward Bond, letter to Calum MacCrimmon, 6 March 1989.

46 Edward Bond, letter to Calum MacCrimmon, 6 March 1989.

47 Bond *War* 306.

48 Bond introduction 29.

49 Edward Bond, "Notes on 'Theatre Events,'" 4 January 1990.

50 Bond introduction 36 & 37.

51 Edward Bond, "Notes to Actors of 'September.'"

52 Edward Bond, lecture given to the National Association of Drama Conference, October 1989. Transcript in *The Fight for Drama–The Fight for Education*, NATD conference, ed. Ken Byron, April 1990. 20.

53 "September" 7.

54 "September" 7.

55 Bond introduction 25.

56 Edward Bond, letter to John Chandler, 7 December 1989.

57 Edward Bond, personal interview, 14 December 1989.

58 Edward Bond, personal interview, 14 December 1989.

59 Jim Hiley, *Listener*, 8 August 1985.

60 Hiley.

61 Edward Bond, letter to author, 1 July 1985.

62 Ian McDiarmid, personal interview, 25 September 1989.

63 Edward Bond, interview with Calum MacCrimmon, undated.

64 Edward Bond, letter to author, 1 July 1985.

65 Edward Bond, interview with Calum MacCrimmon, undated.

66 Edward Bond, letter to Margaret Eddershaw, 4 April 1990.

67 David Shaw-Parker, personal interview, 11 September 1989.

68 Maggie Steed, personal interview, 9 October 1989. *The War Plays* were usually presented in two sections: Parts One and Two were shown the same evening with Part Three taking place the subsequent evening. *Red Black and Ignorant* lasted approximately one hour and ten minutes; *The Tin Can People* one hour and thirty-five minutes and *Great Peace* was approximately three and a half hours in length.

69 Edward Bond, interview with Calum MacCrimmon, undated.

70 Bond *War* 2.

71 Stewart Laing, personal interview, 3 May 1990.

72 Edward Bond, personal interview, 14 December 1989.

73 Stewart Laing, personal interview, 3 May 1990.

74 "Silence" is reprinted in *Edward Bond Poems 1978-1985* (London: Methuen, 1987) 274.

75 Edward Bond, taped correspondence, November 1983.

76 "September" 2.

77 Since *The War Plays*, Bond has not allowed any premieres of his work at the RSC.

Chapter Six

Jackets

Written in 1988, produced in 1989 and published in 1990, *Jackets* is split into two parts; the first set in eighteenth century Japan, the second a city in "modern Europe." Like *The War Plays* trilogy, the work can be performed as a whole or separated into two independent plays, *Jackets I* and *II*.

The first complete production of *Jackets* was given by students on January 24, 1989 at the Department of Theatre Studies, University of Lancaster, to commemorate the twenty-fifth anniversary of the University's founding. Although the play was directed by Keith Sturgess, Head of Department, Bond assisted in the production process. The play was presented as a double-bill at the Nuffield Studio in Lancaster on three evenings January 24-26, 1989.

The professional premiere of *Jackets II* took place at The University of East Anglia, Norwich, England, on October 23, 1989, with the company also presenting rehearsed readings of the first play. This production was a touring production from the Education and Outreach Department at the Haymarket Theatre, Leicester, which performed at twenty-five different locations in the English Midlands until November 24, 1989. *Jackets II* was then staged at the Studio in the Haymarket Theatre, Leicester, from November 28 until December 9, 1989. After these performances, the production went into re-rehearsal on February 12, 1990, with its London premiere on February 27, 1990 at the Bush Theatre. Directed by Nick Philippou, the Leicester production received substantial assistance and cooperation from Bond during rehearsals and the play's London transfer.

Jackets I is based on "The Village School," a scene from Takeda Izumo's (and other authors) Japanese play *Sugawara's*

Secrets of Calligraphy. Written for the Bunraku, or puppet the-atre, it was adapted shortly afterwards for the kabuki. "The Vil-lage School" is often performed independently and was the inspiration for John Masefield's play, *The Pine*. Under the title of *Bushido*, "The Village School" was performed in the USA dur-ing the early part of the twentieth century.[1] In Bond's version, Matsuo and Chiyo, people of "good breeding," leave their son, Kotaro, at the house of the schoolmaster, Genzo, and his wife, Tonami. Henba, leader of an alternative movement within the feudal power struggle, has commanded the Emperor's son, Kan Shu, to be beheaded. He believes Kan Shu to be at the school-master's house which is the case. Desperate to provide Henba, who will not recognise the Emperor's son, with a boy's head, Genzo kills Kotaro. In doing so, they are unaware of the boy's identity or that Matsuo, Chiyo and Kotaro had known they would sacrifice the boy's life to save the Emperor's son. Matsuo, who has taught archery to Kan Shu, is brought by Henba to identify his own son's severed head as that of the prince. This he does, despite the extremity of his suffering, and the Emperor's son is saved. Subsequently, war breaks out.

Jackets II, by contrast set in modern Europe, examines the different worlds and outlooks of Brian Tebham, an army pri-vate, and Phil Lewis, a member of the civilian resistance. The city is in a state of civil unrest and the army are searching for an excuse to increase military operations. With the knowledge of an army Padre, Private Tebham's murder is arranged, the death of a soldier being a justification for increased "protect-ion" of the city. Tebham's contact and eventual killer happens to be Phil Lewis, who opposes the army. Such a confrontation between two friends forces Brian to see how a capitalist society operates to the advantage of a particular class. Realizing he cannot turn back, Brian shoots himself. Phil covers him with a stolen jacket, taken during the riots, and this leads to a confu-sion of identity. Mrs Lewis is asked to identify her dead son's corpse. Mrs Tebham, present to support her friend, discovers the body to be that of Brian.

Parallels exist between *Jackets I* and *II* which, when the plays are presented together, emerge as a powerful indictment of any society that impels sacrifice for an unjust cause. In *Jackets I*,

Matsuo and Chiyo believe they sacrificed their son. However, Kotaro has overheard them arranging his death and so dies with full knowledge of their intentions. Similarly, Brian takes his own life in *Jackets II*. The boys' mothers, Chiyo and Mrs Tebham, are also forced into making a sacrifice by the loss of their son's lives. But at the center of both plays is an expression of Bond's horror over what he sees as the dangerous conditioning taking place in society. For example, in Japan, prolonging Kan Shu's life results in Kotaro's death and, in *Jackets II*, Brian commits suicide. The difference between these two deaths is that Bond sees Kotaro's death as wasted but Brian's as a growth in understanding—Brian has recognized that without his sacrifice the system cannot be changed. Such action is foreshadowed by Tygo's mother from the first play, strongly reminiscent of the Woman in *Great Peace*, who comments on the absurdity of the situation:

> World come to its end t'day. Ont no respect t'stay on your knees an' let it pass! (*Goes to the other women*) If you're the mothers of kids. . .? (*She holds out her hand in the gesture she used to HENBA. No response.*) Ont goo empty handed. Cows roarin'—old people cryin'—dads cursin! But no lads hollerin in the fields: whole world seem empty! Why're you so hard? Where'll it end if the common people fight your wars?[2]

The speech contains both a challenge and warning; the need to apprehend the workings of a capitalist society on the edge of war and to act on this understanding before human life is lost. It is in the Canal Path scene of *Jackets II*, that Phil describes an episode from the rioting in the city and explains to Brian the implications of his actions:

> Tailor's dummy on the stairs. Evenin jacket. Tried it on! Another dummy in the mirror: by the rails. Got a leather jacket. Went over. Bent down. Not a dummy: bloke trying it on—shot in the stomach. I was in an evenin jacket strippin a corpse an there's a war goin on in the street. You cant live like that!. . . What's worse?—lootin for them or working for them? Working for them!—so they can loot us! That's the crime—an it screws up all the rest! You're not 'ere t' stop us lootin'—you're 'ere because *we* want *our* lives.[3]

Both of these alternative visions of the world, expressed by the Mother and Phil, reject easy alternatives. The Mother of *Jackets I* attempts to goad people into action by evoking an austere vision of an empty world. However, Phil describes a society torn apart, but goes one stage further than Tygo's Mother; he states explicitly that it is in the establishment's political and economic interest to suppress civil disobedience. As a result of this insight Brian realizes that he must die.

Some incidents of the first play have resonances in the second. For example, Genzo's display of his robe, showered with Kotaro's blood, foreshadows the Policeman's exposition of the jacket in *Jackets II*. In *Jackets I*, Chiyo is almost certain that what she sees is her son's blood; in *Jackets II*, Mrs Lewis responds in a similar way to what she believes to be Phil's blood. The distinction between *Jackets I* and *II* is, ironically, that the blood on the jacket in the second play belongs to an anonymous individual, with fresh stains made by Brian's blood as he shoots himself. The image of blood was emphasized by Bond insisting, for the Lancaster production, that Genzo enter covered by "a whole sheet of blood."[4] In *Jackets I* and *II*, blood is also connected to an animal-like instinct of both women. For instance Chiyo's reaction is that she "smells" Kotaro's blood on Genzo's robe and in *Jackets II* Mrs Lewis recoils from the jacket because she "can smell the blood from 'ere."[5] The relief experienced by Mrs Lewis, on discovering that her son is alive, is also like the mixed emotions of Matsuo and Chiyo on learning of Kotaro's death, changing masks as they alternate between joy and grief. Central to both *Jackets I* and *II*, are the characters' extreme reactions. Apart from its undoubted theatrical effectiveness, Bond hopes that by showing his characters' suffering an audience will understand more accurately what, in his opinion, is the cause of such responses—a capitalist society that encourages violence and misery.

Bond has stated that *Jackets* needs performing in its entirety to show the broadness and completeness of the plays' vision.[6] This is a view shared by Maureen Morris, the actress who played Mrs Lewis in the Leicester/London production:

> I feel if only we had done both plays, Bond would not be getting the hammering he is now. I think the two plays together add up to one of the most remarkable pieces in the theatre.[7]

Since this study primarily concerns itself with the productions of *Jackets II*, it is important to explore the characters in this play who run society, such as the Officer and Padre, and those, like Brian, Phil, Mrs Lewis and Mrs Tebham, who are run by it.

The Officer understands the workings of society but, as it operates to his advantage, does nothing to change it. In performance, Bond stipulates the same actor must play the Officer and Brian. Technically this needs to occur as both characters must look alike. But it is also Bond's most direct parallel between the sacrificer and sacrificed in this play. Such coupling strongly suggests the two sides of human behavior, both men have the potential to act violently and peacefully. For Bond, the difference in response is based purely along class lines. The Officer is representative of a figure head, the upper class, although it is deeply ironical that, as a soldier in the field, the Officer is incapable of actually exercising his power. Brian, like Bob of *Restoration*, represents the working classes, who are inevitably exploited and go to their death. Such doubling sets up interesting parallels for an actor. This was a point made by the director of *Jackets II* in Leicester and London, Nick Philippou:

> What does it mean for an actor who has been playing the corpse on a stretcher to come back on stage as another character and say, almost to an audience, "When we bring an army in, it will be as safe as anesthetizing a corpse."[8]

The Padre, like the Officer, is also representative of the upper-class. His dislike of the working class and consequent ridicule of them echoes many characteristics of the Parson and Lord Are from *Restoration*.

Brian and Phil are two friends caught on opposite sides of the class war. Brian is an unfortunate pawn trapped in the game waged by those such as the Officer. As with Bob in *Restoration* and the Son of *Great Peace*, Brian attempts to fulfill the wishes of the upper class; in this case he becomes a soldier and, in Bond's terms, is exploited by another class. Brian is taken advantage of and this loyalty is seen to cost him his life. Phil, like Rose in *Restoration*, understands the way society is structured but unlike Brian does not seek "acceptable" solutions. In the final scene, Bond gives him the simple action to "carefully change from slippers to street shoes."[9] This can be interpreted as an optimistic sign, comparable to Len mending the chair in the final scene of *Saved*; it is an indication that the battle is to go on. In performances in London, Bond introduced the irony of the Officer handing Phil his shoes as he prepared to leave. This gesture suggests that the establishment assists in subverting the very structure which it itself imposes.

One of the play's more unsettling moments comes when Mrs Lewis becomes mentally disturbed over Brian's death and fails to recognize his corpse. Under the circumstances, Mrs Lewis initially behaves rationally in this scene, her anger and sorrow remaining in proportion to the Policeman's insensitivity and the extremity of the situation. On realizing that the body is not her son's, the joy Mrs Lewis experiences turns to uncontrollable laughter. This might be understandable, laughter being a release for her prolonged inner tension. However the inappropriateness of Mrs Lewis's laughter, on realizing the body to be Brian Tebham, causes an uneasy response. It is similar to Clare's laughter in the cell scene of *The Fool*, a moment in which Clare, like Mrs Lewis, also covers himself with a blanket.[10] In *Jackets II*, this incident could be defined as a typical TE—an insight into the minds of the characters which can only occur in the theatre. At this moment Bond captures the relationship of Mrs Lewis to the corpse, turning it into an extreme emotional response which forces an audience into understanding the horror of the situation.

Death dominates the play as, according to Mrs Lewis, Mrs Tebham has been dead throughout and what an audience witnesses in the final scene, is her emerging awareness of her responsibilities as an individual. The actress playing Mrs Tebham in the Leicester and London production, Janette Legge, commented on this moment:

> Mrs Lewis says to Mrs Tebham in the last scene, "You died too—but *you* came back," Mrs Tebham looks at Brian's corpse and accepts what she sees, Mrs Lewis looks and she does not see. Mrs Tebham is in hell but does not get swallowed up by it. She has one look at Mrs Lewis to say she is not mad. It is like when people are at the centre of themselves.[11]

In *Jackets I*, the mother, who could be closely associated with Mrs Tebham, prophetically comments; "'Stead he comes up with new rubbish! Say the army'll teach 'un t' do tricks! More likely how t' git blow t' bits!"[12] At the end of *Jackets II*, Mrs Tebham is forced into rebuilding her world with the increased knowledge and understanding gained as a result of Brian's death.

As stated in connection with *The Woman*, in Bond's theory of theatre, Theatre Events are nothing new; their importance, in Bond's concept of theatre, lies in the analysis they provide:

> If naturalism itself becomes the object of drama, then there is no analysis. I find this problem in Chekhov, from whom I learned much. He uses TEs just as I do—but they are not analytical.[13]

Bond comments on the function of a TE and its relevance to life outside the theatrical environment:

> You can look at a telephone box abstractly. But this isnt done when you use it to phone for an ambulance or announce a birth. Then the phone box—when it is seen—does have a changed appearance—a "happening" appearance: but it isnt abstract—it makes demands on the spectator. What is then seen is the thing's or the event's—social meaning. This makes the meaning immanent. Seen abstractly the thing or event would have a transcendental meaning. But birth is not transcendental—it is the entry into the ordinary. And death is not transcendental.[14]

Margaret Eddershaw, who played Chiyo at Lancaster, describes a link between theory and practice in the "use" of TEs:

> Heads are important in this play . . . so what Edward had Phil doing, at the beginning of the second act, was crouching behind the table so his head would appear isolated from his body. It was extremely odd, totally bewildering to the actor. We may not have done this in the end.[15]

Eddershaw maintains that a number of images, which could operate as TEs, occur within the play:

> There is the wrapping up of Kotaro's body and the unwrapping of Brian's. Also repeated images about blood. There is a kind of ritual element in the first play, echoed in the second, which makes connections on a different, almost poetic, level which works, subconsciously for an audience.[16]

In *Jackets* a TE can be of two forms; occurring within the play itself or a form imposed on the text from outside. The saucer of tea in the last scene of *Jackets II* is a specific Theatre Event taking place within the play, and so is the jacket in the penultimate scene. But a TE can also be applied to a scene externally during rehearsals. One example of connected images in performance was the mechanical movement of Brian as he shot himself and of Mrs Lewis as she saw the body at the Police Station. Bond hopes the sustained images of a character being momentarily mechanistic will help an audience connect these two incidents. Theoretically this means attention will focus on the occurrence's cause and effect. In rehearsals at the Bush Theatre, London, Bond communicated to the actress that the circular movement of her hands should not, in anyway, express motion. Initially held to the side of her head as she performed this action, her hands continued the rolling action made by the trolley on which the corpse lay. In performance this action was deleted, Mrs Lewis instead slowly rolling down her spine and moving downstage holding her loose arms by her side. Although she admitted to not understanding this moment completely, Maureen Morris was able to communicate the attitude of Mrs Lewis:

> I am sort of in shock and I don't think it is necessary to understand it, it is really an audience picture and then that sort of geyser of laughter comes bubbling out. . . I use the gesture as a bridge from one moment of the scene to another.[17]

Morris interprets the Police Station scene as a turning point for Mrs Lewis. In her opinion, three contrasting sides are shown; the anxious mother, the laughing woman and, finally, the beginning of the character's derangement shown in the last scene. Such an interpretation is significant because it demonstrates a naturalistic interpretation of the character often antithetical to Bond's techniques:

> Mrs Lewis has a kind of flamboyance, a show of confidence, and that is attacked in the middle scene and completely opposed in the last scene. It is like being three characters which is wonderful as an actress because you have got an enormously broad canvas to paint on.[18]

In preparation for the London production, the Padre used a pistol to show Tebham where he could be shot. Bond had suggested this idea in correspondence to Philippou:

> In rehearsals it might be useful if the Padre actually held the pistol—and showed it to the soldier—and used it to point to the best targets—and handed it back to the soldier when he said: I leave the details to you. Its like selling an upholstery brush. Curiously enough if too much is psychologically invested in these interchanges they lose interest and also the character isnt explained.[19]

This rehearsal exercise with the gun might have formed another TE although the weapon was not used in performance.

> I like this idea of teaching. I remembered the other day how I was taught to use a gun. It was all by numbers. Killing by numbers. I don't know that you need to use the gun in performance, perhaps you don't need it now. It's just to get you into the idea of actually showing him where he could be shot. He is driven to being that specific. This is the humour that each time he is driven to spelling it out in great detail. The appalling clarity.[20]

A connection was also made in the London revival between Phil's removal of the stolen clothes from the bag at the beginning of *Jackets II* and the Policeman's removal of Phil's jacket during Scene F. The repetition of this gesture, removing the clothes from the bag, reminds an audience of their origin: obtained by Phil during the riots. In notebooks, Bond observes the parallel he is making:

> Phil carried a big plastic bag (probably a bin liner) and he then spills from it onto the floor a heap of clothes: later the Policeman will take the jacket from a bag. This isn't making futile "patterns"—its a way of asking people to understand their actions; that political disasters dont come from outside life, but within the *way* we live.[21]

Bond also comments on the similarity between the Policeman's removal of the jacket from the bag and Mrs Lewis's folding of the sheet at the end of the scene:

> The careful folding of the sheet contrasts with the way clothes are tipped from the bin liner at the start. The way the Policeman removes the jacket from the sack combines both—it is brutal—but mechanically very efficient. These boxes of patterns demonstrate how the social shapes existence.[22]

Jackets II, in its London production, contained a number of moments where the tension was exploited between a "reality" of the situation and its wider social meaning; for example, the significance of the dress looted from the shops by Phil and Mrs Tebham's initial reaction to it. Bond's comments during rehearsals indicate its importance and function as a TE:

> The dress should suggest all the things Mrs Tebham has never been able to have. It has to be a moment of self- understanding... For example, your hands when you touch it, they should be fists. It's not the dress that you wear, its the attitude to the dress. The dress goes on, something happens and you blame them. This should be one of those incredible moments in the theatre, Hedda Gabler burns the book. Here is this woman tearing up the most precious thing on stage.[23]

The response of Mrs Tebham to the dress is important. In rehearsal, Bond went to great lengths to emphasize that, despite Mrs Tebham's initial reluctance, she does try the dress on. Bond indicated that, "for a moment she believes it is possible to have miracles."[24] The reality of her disappointment though is clear once she puts on the dress. Bond helped the actress find this moment by having Mrs Tebham weep once she tries the dress on. In performance, Janette Legge, made a gesture of agony once she is dressed in the stolen garment, giving herself the illusion that the material was "covered with fish-scales."[25] Her reaction jolted the audience causing both laughter at the situation and providing a moment of social insight. The dress was also significant in the Lancaster production, Eddershaw recalling the moment as a curious mixture of styles:

> It was about Mrs Tebham's reaction, whether she feels uncomfortable or embarrassed, really likes it but daren't express it. In the Police Station, the whole scene is grotesque. But the moment of the dress is quite real. It is an understandable situation. It is a realistic situation. It is the Brechtian principle of making the familiar strange.[26]

Bond considers this an important "T" moment, having wider implications throughout the play:

> The gesture you make of delight and surprise when you pick something up from the beach—even from a distance it reads "found:" the finding and the gesture—the found object and the gesture—are joined in one

analysis. We need to relate the dress incident to the cell incident. . .
She, if you like, emotionally remembers the first incident: though I'd
rather say that it had become part of her and so didnt even need
remembering, it was there when needed. Whether a woman would in
fact say such a thing in the cell isnt important—this woman would—
because of the dress. A few moments later she shudders and says that
the walls are dressed with live paint. Isnt that something to do with
what she felt when she put the dress on?—that somehow it was alive—
had the lives of wasted labour in it.[27]

In notes to the cast in London, Bond requested they not
"normalize" or "naturalize" these TEs or change their playing
over the production's four week's duration. He stated, "Be bold
and arrogant about these "T" events because then you will
excite an audience."[28]

Metaphors were also used as TEs and given practical exploration in both rehearsals and performance. An action appearing in the text, but not executed in the Leicester production,
was the Padre's self-flagellation with his cap at the end of Scene
C. Bond describes the importance of this gesture:

There is a moment when the psychology becomes very raw. The text
says the Padre beats himself with a cap. In performance this wasnt
done. Yet there is something surprising and analytical about the gesture. The Padre uses the symbol of authority to attack his legs. This
should be a surprising and frightening moment.[29]

The image was restored in the London production and became
a moment of insight into the workings of the Padre's mind.
Bond likens this incident to Mrs Lewis at the Police Station
stuffing the sheet/shroud into her mouth. "Her mouth is a
dead place, haunted by the laughter of ghosts—because her
mind has not seen her 'son' and therefore not herself."[30] Both
incidents are intended to alienate an audience from the realm
of naturalistic observation. But the question remains how to
translate this analysis into practical theatre action. By way of
answering this, Bond made significant efforts to give definition
and shape to his alternative concept of "T" acting for both *Jackets I* and *II* in Lancaster and *Jackets II* in Leicester and London.

"T" acting is a unique approach to character, an ideological
extension of ideas from Bond's *Activists Papers*, expressed by the
phrase, "Possess the character don't let it possess you."[31] Bond

has described the job of playing a character as complex and created a useful image for explaining his concept of performance:

> I would say you have to play a character as a departmental store. . . That is there are lots of different departments and they all are absolutely necessary; there is somewhere you go to get clothes, food, recreational things. It's as if to play a character you have to say, "Which department am I in at the moment?" And then you play that ruthlessly.[32]

In notebooks, Bond states more specifically the purpose of his alternative approach to acting:

> As so often in acting, its a case of showing us the parcel and not whats in it. Contents can be—have to be—shown later. It needs authority to show the parcel. Its wrong on stage to always want to be the letterwriter sometimes its important to be the postman. One reason for this is that it shows the social role, how society exists in the character.[33]

Bond suggests that with "T" acting an actor plays the outer manifestation of a character and slowly reveals an individual's social make up. An example of "T" acting occurred in *Jackets II*, Scene F., where Mrs Tebham inspects the corpse. It successfully links the theory of "T" acting to the play. At Lancaster, Mrs Tebham's expression froze as she looked at the corpse's face; whereas in London, Mrs Tebham looked towards Mrs Lewis once before returning to the corpse. Both approaches attempt to communicate more than just the interior sorrow of a mother. As Bond has stated:

> If at this moment we show only that the mother is upset, we havent shown much: we've shown that mothers get upset when they're face to face with their dead sons. We know that. We ought to show how society has killed the son. How it has put the woman into the unthinkable situation.[34]

Bond's concept of "T" acting dominated the Leicester/London production and Scene D of *Jackets II*, took a new departure. In a letter, Bond advises Philippou:

> All the characters in the short street scene should be in farce; The scene shouldnt be played for sympathy by anyone. The army has put them in this farcical situation.[35]

This tone was captured in both rehearsal and performance. In rehearsal Philippou played the scene with actors attempting to extend their roles to extremes; the Padre playing a demonic priest desperate for a dead body. Phil, a caricature villain and Brian the innocent hero who befriended the audience in his aside about wearing ties. In performance some of this extremity was retained. The Padre's attempts at "proving" to himself and the audience that there had been a miracle provoked laughter by his urgent and insistent manner.

Bond often uses regional dialects for his characters. In *Jackets II* the dialect broadly fits into two groups: the Officer and the Padre share a polished accent whereas Brian, Phil, the Policeman, Mrs Tebham and Mrs Lewis speak in a direct English working class dialect. Although there was little dialect work in rehearsals for either production of *Jackets*, it is an important consideration in production. Bond has commented that "language shouldn't be just words, it should be something that moves in the mouth and forces gesture and forces action."[36]

Other practical measures employed for the London production were aimed at stimulating the actors. Cicely Berry, voice coach for the RSC, held a workshop for the Padre and the Officer/Brian. Bond's complex language in the play often meant that actors often lost sight of the characters' original intentions. Berry's workshop was an attempt to return the actors to their political needs by focussing their attention on the words they used. For example, one exercise involved both actors speaking a speech while moving between chairs on each punctuation mark. Another was drawing a picture whilst a speech was in progress, an exercise designed to distract the actors' attention and remind them of the ease with which they could handle the words. Finally Berry devised an exercise to assist the actors in clarifying intentions. Both spoke the "subtext" of their character in Scene B. What became evident was that Bond hardly created a subtext; characters' intentions lay on the surface, being apparent in what they said. In addition, the exercise was useful in identifying the rivalry between the two characters causing Bond to remark, "one realizes how much competition there is."[37] The workshop also created the correct atmosphere for "T" acting. By concentrating on the externals of a character, their language, movement and gesture, Berry was able to distance the actors from any anxiety over inner motivations.

During rehearsals for *Jackets* at Leicester, Bond stressed the importance of the play's conclusion. Despite the scene's apparent bleakness, he stated that there should be a sense of expectancy, of hope in the final image. This was an element emphasized by Mrs Lewis and Mrs Tebham sitting and looking at the audience as the lights dimmed. In effect it was similar to the conclusion of *The Sea*, where Willy's incomplete line suggests the need "for the audience to go away and complete the sentence in their own lives."[38] But for Bond, the importance of "T" acting is that it clarifies the play's structure for an audience in political terms.

Before considering the production's physical elements, it is important to introduce the concept of "another world" described by Bond in relation to *Jackets II*. This is essentially a shift in gear felt as Bond rehearsed the play in Leicester. According to Bond, the "other world" is experienced when the crisis is so demanding "that this forces them into another world."[39] Two examples can be given, the first of which is Mrs Tebham's desire to inflict suffering on another woman prior to her friend's identification of the corpse:

> Perhaps the lad'll belong t'some other woman—goin on with 'er work and doesnt know what she's got in front of 'er. I 'ope she forgives us when she suffers. What else can we do?: I 'ope when her time comes the pain's so sharp she cries out!—so she 'as t'see why we were too weak to bear it an 'ad to push it on to someone else.[40]

Bond commented on this moment:

> Mrs Tebham hopes the pain will be so great that the other woman will be forced to understand. Normally the character would say she hopes the pain wont be too bad: but its as if she knows that would be a sentimental compromise, because then she herself might be moral, the pain must be more severe . . . and then you are into another world of reference, where actions and words have a new integrity and responsibility.[41]

Once he understands his situation, Brian's suggestion that Phil shoot him is a further example of how the play lifts onto another level of reality.

In rehearsals at the Bush, London, Bond asked Tom Hudson, playing Brian, to consider the change from defiance about his death to pleading for it. In performance, the actor took a long pause while he adjusted to this new form of thinking. The separation into "reality" and the "other world" occurs in much of Bond's drama, especially in later work. In *The War Plays* Bond drives his characters forward relentlessly, until the point is reached where they cannot turn back. They have to "accept the responsibilities":

> This is Macbeth's reflection, that he's come so far he would find it as tedious to go back as go on—but Macbeth is making excuses, he must go on in order to become what he is.[42]

In an interview, Bond considers that it was during rehearsals of *Jackets* in 1989, he first recognized the significance of the "other world" stressing that this discovery is one of the reasons he likes directing his own work:

> Once you cross that barrier very strange things become possible. Very often what happens . . . is that things become very extreme. They are in a new world and behave and act differently. Actions have a practical effect on the structures of society. If you are living in a concentration camp then you are living in another world.[43]

During the tour and production of *Jackets II* and its subsequent performances in London, there was one cast change. Maggie Ford, the actress playing Mrs Lewis, left the company after the tour and Maureen Morris, who had previously appeared as Mrs Tebham, took the part. The role of Mrs Tebham was assumed by Janette Legge, four days prior to the play's opening at Leicester. Playing both Mrs Lewis and Mrs Tebham, gave Morris a unique insight into the world of these different women. Only in performance does the extent of their relative strength and weakness become clear, both characters being the opposite of what appears on the page. By playing both characters, Morris was able to be extra-sensitive to Mrs Tebham's limitations compared to Mrs Lewis, and to how the latter character changes during the play:

> One of the things that worried me about Mrs Tebham is that she made a very significant but a very minute journey in the play. The difference

between her in scene one and the last scene for instance is quite profound, but not very noticeable. . . Whereas with Mrs Lewis I really
enjoyed finding out those little things, painting my toenails red, that
kind of flamboyance.[44]

The setting for the production was simple, the whole play, at
Leicester and London, occurring in front of white screens covered with indiscriminate splashes of blue and orange. The floor
cloth, covering the whole stage, was a textured orange. In both
productions the lighting was a bright white light and, as previously mentioned with many of Bond's other productions, the
break between scenes was lit. This was a convention initially
observed at Leicester, although suspended for fear of making
the situation unclear. It was reintroduced in London on the
wishes of both Bond and Philippou.

Tom Hudson, playing Brian, was unsure whether this lighting
technique worked in the theatre: "If it went black after Brian
shoots himself then the power of the scene remains with the
audience. Before they know it they are in a police cell."[45] In
naturalistic terms there is an argument against lighting Brian's
exit. One critic commented:

I was surprised by the director's decision following Brian Tebham's
marvelously convincing death in agony from the bullet wound, to make
the actor stand up and walk off stage ready for the next scene, ruining
the impact of his powerful performance.[46]

However, Philippou's arguments for lighting the interval
between scenes was that it demystified the audience's experience, reminding them that they were just watching actors at
work on a stage. This notion permeated the acting style.
Throughout, actors entered the space as actors, adopting their
character positions before the full brightness of the scene. In
Bond's opinion it was "very exciting" to watch Hudson die as a
character and then exit as an actor, it was part of the "liberation
of theatre."[47]

This production of *Jackets II* included four songs given piano
and guitar accompaniment by the company. The actor playing
Phil sang "D'You Think I'll Always Carry Your Load?" from the
first part, two of the verses being sung between Section B and
C and the last two at the end of C. The women and Phil sang

"The Broken Cup" between Sections A and B. Bond wrote two new songs to be performed at Leicester and subsequently in London. "The Song of Two Mothers," sung by the actresses playing Mrs Tebham and Mrs Lewis between sections D and E and between Sections F and G. "Children Sit Bowed at Your School Desks" was omitted.

Using music in his plays, Brecht wanted to keep an audience conscious at all times:

> [At concert halls] . . . we see entire rows of human beings transported into a peculiar doped state, wholly passive, sunk without trace, seemingly in the grip of a severe poisoning that these people are the helpless and involuntary victims of the unchecked lurching of their emotions.[48]

Bond would agree with these sentiments but is unsure whether Brecht's musical technique is conducive to fulfilling a new dramatic function.

As with the total visual experience, Bond is concerned that his music should be an additional theatrical element, used not only to comment, but more importantly to startle. In a letter, Bond discusses the potential use of music in his plays:

> Now music does not alienate or even comment—but instructs. Of course much music does in fact comment, but the dramatic moments— the moments of meaning and value the music is internalised [into the play] and imposes value and meaning.[49]

The program at Leicester contained a short commentary by Tony Coult about Bond's work as a writer and a copy of "The Broken Cup Song." In London, these were replaced by a new poem, "Europe," written by Bond on remarkable structural changes in Europe and Bond wanted to reflect these in a song by Mrs Tebham. Due to restricted rehearsal time this was not possible, so instead the lyrics appeared in the program. In two seven line stanzas punctuated by a chorus, "Europe" challenges the assumption that society will be radically changed by the shifts in power occurring throughout the world:

> The old questions still arent answered
> The old problems dont go away
> O Europe—you have so many dead
> To answer to on resurrection day[50]

Despite alterations to society's organisation, in Bond's opinion the central difficulty and injustices of class division remain. Until those are solved, every solution must be temporary:

> The broken bricks of the Berlin Wall do not stop being a wall simply because they are carried away and spread far and wide in thousands of hands. The hands make them a wall. Its never been more important or more interesting to write: mistakes in writing have never been more dangerous or more ridiculous or dirtier.[51]

Prior to the tour of *Jackets II* in October 1989 Bond gave his first interview to the press in over two years. A number of reporters were present at this press conference and the interview was subsequently carried by *Leicester Mercury*.

In discussing the significance of *Jackets* to the working class, Bond stresses the value of drama in promoting understanding:

> An artist must not be bland and make excuses. I want to take ordinary people to the very limits of their experience—I want to give people back their dignity.[52]

This comment is consistent with Bond's more general thought about the use individuals may make of this play:

> I would like to feel that I might contact the people who dont usually go to the theatre, and that it would become a tool for them, something that people can use. What I want this to do, is for people to say—look, Im seeing on stage a human person with problems, laughing over his problems, lying over them, being honest. It's an experience that can make my problems practical for me; I can develop a practical relationship to the stage.[53]

Prior to the production's London opening in 1990, the *Times* carried a profile on Bond by Jim Hiley. One reason the article is important is that it situates the source of conflict between Bond and his actors in their differing approaches to character:

> For most British performers, their work is a subjective process, centering on the question: "What is my character feeling now?" Bond's preoccupation is the place of an individual in a changing world.[54]

By attending rehearsals and developing his concepts of TE and "T" acting, Bond tried to foster an attitude of a socially responsible actor, an actor committed to his character, the production and, most importantly, to the wider impact of the play.

The production of *Jackets* at Lancaster attempted to forge links between the first and second parts of the play. This was initially conceived by Sturgess through the set, lighting design and the casting used in both plays:

> It is a complex experience having the two plays back to back. The connections have to be made ever so carefully. I think from a directorial point of view it was not clear to me how much pointing should go on. I didn't know whether I should be making clear and obvious parallels between the two plays.[55]

Sturgess directed the production at the University's Nuffield Studio, which is equipped with a revolving stage. The division between the two worlds of *Jackets I* and *II* was accentuated by a series of flats running across the space:

> On one side they looked like Japanese sliding doors/screens. There were six or seven of these and they provided entrances and exits for the actors. . . An air of mystery was created too, you were never quite sure what was happening on the other side of the screen. . . The other side was a more complicated shape and instead of screens there were doors. I also had a little furniture. The odd filing cabinet, the occasional dressing of the set. But all the elements were about holding information and releasing it. It was not an attempt at realism but these things reminiscent of modern society rather than the Japanese school. It was painted a rather horrid institutional green and, I think, the floor was black.[56]

Selected to create a connection between *Jackets I* and *II*, the production's physical elements were quite complicated. This emphasis Bond disliked and he attempted to delete what he considered unnecessary. For example, Bond wanted to remove the appearance of Kotaro's head from the box:

> He did not want that because, he said, "the audience will titter, they always do when Macbeth's head is brought on." . . . Somehow we managed to keep the head in and the audience did not move. I thought that unless the head was there the test for the father was incomplete.[57]

Bond believes theatrical illusions are unnecessary and intrusive when a point can be made in a way that an audience can interpret consciously.

In an attempt to resolve the potential problem of an audience seeing the two plays as being "only casually put together,"
Sturgess played *Jackets I* and *II* with the same cast. At Lancaster,
Margaret Eddershaw playing Chiyo also played Mrs Tebham
and Amanda Hadingue, as Tonami, played Mrs Lewis. This
casting was also adopted by Nick Philippou at the Leicester
readings of *Jackets I*. There was further doubling in the production, but the casting, of Chiyo/Tebham, Tonami/Lewis, was a
conscious attempt to link the notion of sacrifice in both plays.

Musically the production was simple. The songs were set to
music by an ex-postgraduate student from the University and
played by a separate small ensemble although sung by members
of the company. "Children Sit Bowed at Your School Desks"
was sung by the school children at the beginning of *Jackets I*,
"D'You Think I'll Always Carry Your Load?" was sung after
Kotaro's body was carried out and before the Emperor's son
asked "What d'you want?" Bond's stage direction in the script
emphasizes that "the Mother sits alone on stage. It is important
she does not take part in the song." "The Broken Cup," the
third and final song in this production, occurred after Part 2,
[A]. Sturgess had difficulty with the placing of the songs within
the play and consequently was unsure about their purpose: "I
felt uneasy about them. It was never clear whose they were, the
character's, actor's or Bond's. I would have been as happy
doing the play without them."[58]

Bond was satisfied with the London production of *Jackets II*
although, in his final notes to the cast, he warned the actors
against naturalizing the acting. This, he maintained, would fail
to bring out the play's full dramatic structure. To avoid the
potential problem of standardizing the events, Bond instructed
the actors to "hold onto those things that you find strange. I
don't mean those things you do not understand, but instead
concentrate on how you talk to a corpse."[59] Bond realized that
it was these "strange" occurrences, how a human being reacts
in moments of crisis, that an audience had come to witness. As
an example, Bond described the first scene of *Jackets II*:

One woman in a dress she hates. A boy in a jacket he loves. One
woman, not showing these extravagant things, but attempting to work.

In the middle of this, some strange sound. We can normalise that but it
would lose its drama, its significance. An audience wants to see these
strange things. . .[60]

His advice to the actors was to "be bold and arrogant about
these moments because you will excite an audience":

As you perform the play, go for those moments, relish their
strangeness, relish their oddity, relish their theatre. Give the audience a
sense of their own importance, their lives.[61]

It is very clear that in *Jackets*, Bond was attempting to dramatize
the extra-ordinary in people's lives, using characters and emotions that could easily be understood:

What I want to do in *Jackets* is take the class of people who are
excluded from society, the class of consuming slavery, if you like. The
class who become soldiers and go and get blown to bits in Ireland so
that somebody can be taught at Sandhurst how to train soldiers to go
and kill other people, but also how to abuse terrorists, I want to take
those people who are normally written off, are either seen as the
objects of abuse in *The Sun* or the objects of sentimental appeals to
charity or goodwill . . . and say that what you will find working in those
people is all the experience of Hamlet or of Lear.[62]

Jackets, in Lancaster, Leicester and London, broke new
ground in Bond's theory of acting. It clarified his approach to
"T" acting and TE's, a style that Bond has said he will "live off
for several years and will fuel what I am going to write."[63] But
should a writer direct his own work? In an interview, Peter Hall
commented on Bond as director of his plays:

The debit side is clear: [for Bond directing his plays:] lack of objectivity,
lack of other peoples contribution. On the credit side: you are better
off doing it yourself than having a director you are not in sympathy
with or who does not understand what you are trying to get at. The
best thing, in my view, remains a director and a writer who are married
in the sense that they want to fulfill this play together.[64]

The "marriage" that Hall speaks about is what occurred with
Jackets, allowing Bond to learn of the textual difficulties from
actors but also having someone else shape the process.

Notes

1 Further information in Samuel Leiter's *The Art of Kabuki* (Berkeley: University of California Press, 1979)

2 Edward Bond, "Jackets" or "The Secret Hand" in *Two Post-Modern Plays* (London: Methuen 1990) 49.

3 Bond *Jackets II* 74.

4 Keith Sturgess, personal interview, 19 March 1990.

5 Bond *Jackets I* 43 and Bond *Jackets II* 83.

6 Edward Bond, letter to John Clemo, 12 February 1990, states that *Jackets II* "works on its own" but in subsequent conversations Bond has stated the need for staging the entire play.

7 Maureen Morris, personal interview, 7 March 1990.

8 Nick Philippou, personal interview, 15 December 1989.

9 Bond *Jackets II* 93.

10 Edward Bond, "The Fool," in *Plays: Three* (London: Methuen, 1987) 115.

11 Janette Legge, personal interview, 22 March 1990.

12 Bond *Jackets I* 51.

13 Edward Bond, letter to John Clemo, 9 March 1990.

14 Edward Bond, "A Point of Dramatic Practice," 15 March 1990.

15 Margaret Eddershaw, personal interview, 19 March 1990.

16 Margaret Eddershaw, personal interview, 19 March 1990.

17 Maureen Morris, personal interview, 7 March 1990.

18 Maureen Morris, personal interview, 7 March 1990.

19 Edward Bond, letter to Nick Philippou, 27 January 1990.

20 Edward Bond, letter to Nick Philippou, 27 January 1990.

21 Edward Bond notebooks 32. The entire Edward Bond notebook collection is available on Microfilm from the Doheny Library, University of Southern California.

22 Edward Bond notebooks 56.

23 Edward Bond, rehearsals for *Jackets II*, London 1990.

24 Edward Bond, rehearsals for *Jackets II*, London 1990.

25 Janette Legge, rehearsals for *Jackets II*, London 1990.

26 Margaret Eddershaw, personal interview, 19 March 1990.

27 Edward Bond, letter to author, 23 March 1990.

28 Edward Bond, final notes to the London cast of *Jackets II*, 26 February 1990.

29 Edward Bond, letter to Nick Philippou, 27 January 1990.

30 Edward Bond, letter to Nick Philippou, 27 January 1990.

31 Edward Bond *The Worlds with the Activists Papers* (London: Methuen, 1980) 99.

32 Edward Bond, comments to actors of *The Fool*, British Broadcasting Corporation, 21 February 1990.

33 Edward Bond notebooks 44/5.

34 Edward Bond notebooks 45.

35 Edward Bond, letter to Nick Philippou, 27 January 1990.

36 Edward Bond, interview by Tony Coult, "Plays and Players," 1975 quoted in *Bond: A Study of his Plays* by Malcolm Hay and Philip Roberts. (London: Methuen, 1980) 200.

37 Edward Bond, rehearsals for *Jackets II*, London 1990.

38 Edward Bond, letter to Tom H. Wild, 16 January 1977 quoted in *Bond: A Study of his Plays* 163.

39 Edward Bond, personal interview, 12 June 1990.

40 Bond *Jackets II* 84.

41 Edward Bond, letter to John Chandler, 7 December 1989.

42 Edward Bond, letter to John Chandler, 7 December 1989.

43 Edward Bond, personal interview, 12 June 1990.

44 Maureen Morris, personal interview, 7 March 1990.

45 Tom Hudson, rehearsals for *Jackets II*, London 1990.

46 Fran Bowden, *Mansfield Chad* 8 November 1989: 35.

47 Edward Bond, rehearsals for *Jackets II*, London 1990.

48 Bertolt Brecht, *Brecht on Theatre*, trans, John Willett (London: Methuen, 1986) 89.

49 Edward Bond, letter to John Clemo, 12 February 1990.

50 Edward Bond, "Europe," 14 February 1990.

51 Edward Bond, letter to Max Stafford-Clark, 8 March 1990.

52 Edward Bond *Birmingham Post* 2 November 1989: 12.

53 Edward Bond quoted by Tony Coult, *Background Material for 'Jackets'* 1989: 12.

54 Jim Hiley, *Times* 28 February 1990: 19.

55 Keith Sturgess, personal interview, 19 March 1990.

56 Keith Sturgess, personal interview, 19 March 1990.

57 Keith Sturgess, personal interview, 19 March 1990.

58 Keith Sturgess, personal interview, 19 March 1990.

59 Edward Bond, final notes to the London cast of *Jackets II* 26 February 1990.

60 Edward Bond, final notes to the London cast of *Jackets II* 26 February 1990.

61 Edward Bond, final notes to the London cast of *Jackets II* 26 February 1990.

62 Edward Bond quoted by Tony Coult *Background Material for 'Jackets,'* 1989: 19.

63 Edward Bond, final notes to the London cast of *Jackets II*, 26 February 1990.

64 Peter Hall, personal interview, 17 July 1990.

Postscript

From the time of *The Woman*, Bond's basic theory of acting has been consistent. The actor must apply his concept or interpretation of the dramatic situation to the emotion. It is this concept or interpretation which must be acted and not the emotion of the character. Emotion will arise for the actor as a result of playing the idea, but the emotion is a by-product of the political analysis. For an actor, this means additional work because this is a stage which, according to Bond, is often neglected, the actor going directly for the emotion rather than playing the idea. The National Theatre's production of *The Woman* was an artistic if not economic success. However, even though the production was acclaimed for its clarity and original use of the theatre, it offered little opportunity for Bond to develop a cognate approach toward acting. This was mainly due to insufficient rehearsal time to explore the acting style needed for the play.

During rehearsals for *The Worlds* at Newcastle University in 1979, Bond developed the idea of Public Soliloquy (PS). This concept was formed as Bond recognized the need for an actor's honesty to be channeled through dramatic metaphor into a moment where the character observed and analyzed his political situation. Freed from the financial and time constraints of professional theatre, the premiere of *The Worlds* in Newcastle and the play's subsequent London production provided Bond with his first opportunity to practically explore his acting theory. These productions were useful in Bond's development of a theatrical style and they also met with widespread approval.

Bond's experiments with music in *Restoration* were similarly aimed at indicating a character's awareness of the social situation thus providing distance and perspective for the actor. As with the PS, song broke any naturalistic conventions that may have been inferred, allowing an audience to hear directly an analysis of the character's political circumstances. The 1988 production of *Restoration* developed this distancing notion further, attempting to shake the limitations of the play by introducing the additional contemporary relevance of the "Falkland Song." Both productions satisfied Bond's intention that the play should speak to its audience through a mixture of both period and contemporary styles.

The National Theatre's 1982 production of *Summer* provided Bond with a better opportunity to explore and develop an acting style. In rehearsals for *Summer*, Bond attempted to remove his actors from the naturalistic approach to character and explore the play from a more social standpoint. Despite difficulties with some of the actors, the rehearsal process culminated in a production described by one critic as "the most fascinating . . . to be found in the London theatre."[1] For Mary Poole, Bond's direction demonstrated his mastery of the principle that:

> In the theatre words are spoken and heard, existing as sound and hence in time and space. Within this dimension, the playwright and performers can convey additional levels of sense through silence, tone of voice, rhythm, and the words' connection to gestures of characters and images of action.[2]

In many ways this description looks forward to the TE but this was not a concept Bond developed consciously until some years later.

Although *The War Plays* received a poor critical response and the production was condemned by Bond, it was during rehearsals at the RSC in 1986 that Bond became consciously aware of TEs. The TE is a moment, or series of moments, which can be opened up to illuminate the play's wider social meaning. In *Notes on Postmodernism*, Bond discusses the purpose of a TE:

> Unlike happenings, TEs are a means of analytical understanding. They make clear the cause and consequences of events, collecting the diffuseness of real life into illustration and demonstration.[3]

As discussed in Chapter Six, Bond acknowledges that TEs have always been written into his plays. In the production of *Jackets* at Lancaster, Leicester and London, Bond used the TE approach through his concept of "T" acting:

> Although TEs are abstracted from the play they are also integrated in it as part of the total logic of the performance: really this means that the use of TEs results in a generalised way of acting—"T" acting. "T" acting is not acting limited to a two-dimensional political analysis; it asks more, not less; it shows the audience how they can integrate their understanding of the character into their own life.[4]

Having rejected a naturalistic approach to acting, Bond felt under no obligation to create a "realistic" setting. A common element in all the productions Bond has directed or advised on, is the lack of extraneous scenic elements, properties and costume. Possibly the most "elaborate" setting of the productions explored by this study was created for the Royal Court's production of *Restoration*. But even this was designed so that every part of the set was functional and made a useful contribution to the production. The National Theatre's production of *The Woman* emphasized the vastness of the Olivier auditorium by its absence of set. As Bond has stated this was a conscious choice designed to demonstrate how the conventional stage was usually cluttered with unnecessary props which detracted from, rather than augmented, a play's purpose.

In Bond's opinion, theatre should confront an audience's conventional view of the world, provoking an alternative political insight which is socially useful:

> Productions of my plays should be fiercely dramatic and this means emotional. The emotion is released by the alienation. But if you try to force generalised emotion into my plays (based really on biological reductivism) they become limp and stale. For the actor, the interpretation should combine discipline and creative freedom.[5]

The difficulty faced by Edward Bond is that in attempting to give shape to a theatrical form by directing the first productions of his plays, his primary role as a playwright has been threatened. Many European countries, especially France and Germany, welcome his work. But in Britain, as a result of Bond's directorial intervention, his plays have become marginalized; *Human Cannon* (1985) and *In The Company of Men* (1990) are two plays awaiting their first British professional productions.

Whilst there are a lack of theatres willing or able to create the appropriate settings for experimental work, Bond's reasons for wanting to protect his plays by directing the first productions remain valid.

Notes

1 Mark Amory, *Spectator* 6 February 1982: 28.

2 Mary Poole, "The Dynamic Contradiction in Selected Play of Edward Bond: A Study in Dramatic Technique," diss. Northwestern University, June 1987, 140.

3 Edward Bond, "Notes on Postmodernism," *Two Post-Modern Plays* (London: Methuen, 1990.) 243.

4 Edward Bond, letter to author, 8 October 1990.

5 Edward Bond, letter to author, 8 October 1990.

Works Cited

Primary Sources (Plays)

All sources are unpublished unless an attribution is cited.

Lear (with "Author's Preface.") London: Eyre Methuen, 1972.

The Sea. A Comedy. London: Eyre Methuen, 1973.

Bingo. Scenes of Money and Death. London: Eyre Methuen, 1974.

The Fool. Scenes of Bread and Love. London: Eyre Methuen, 1976.

The Bundle or *New Narrow Road to the Deep North*. Eyre Methuen, 1978.

The Woman. Scenes of War and Freedom. London: Eyre Methuen, 1979.

The Worlds with *The Activists Papers*. London: Eyre Methuen, 1980.

Restoration and *The Cat*. London: Eyre Methuen, 1981.

Summer and *Fables*. London: Methuen, 1982.

Derek with *Choruses from 'After the Assassinations.'* London: Methuen New Theatrescript, 1983.

The War Plays (two vols.) London: Methuen New Theatrescript, 1985.

Restoration London: Methuen, 1988.

September (with "Notes to Actors.") 1989.

Jackets, In The Company of Men with *September* London: Methuen, 1990.

The War Plays London: Methuen, 1991.

Edward Bond Letters I (selected & edited by Ian Stuart) London: Harwood Academic Press, 1994.

Edward Bond Letters II (selected & edited by Ian Stuart) London: Harwood Academic Press, 1995.

Collected Works

Plays: One (with "Author's Note.") London: Eyre Methuen, 1977. (*Saved, Early Morning, The Pope's Wedding*)

Plays: Two (with Introduction and Prefaces.) London: Eyre Methuen, 1982. (*Lear, The Sea, Narrow Road to the Deep North, Black Mass, Passion*)

Plays: Three (with Poems, Short Stories and Essays.) London: Methuen, 1987. (*Bingo, The Fool, The Woman, Stone*).

Plays: Four (with Poems.) London: Methuen, 1992. (*The Worlds, The Activists Papers, Restoration, Summer*).

Theatre Poems and Songs, selected and edited by Malcolm Hay and Philip Roberts. London: Eyre Methuen, 1978.

Other Works

Observer, "Sunday Plus" 15 January 1978, with Victoria Radin. 31.

"On Brecht," *Theatre Quarterly* Vol. VIII no. 30, 1978. 34.

"Us, Our Drama and the National Theatre," *Plays and Players*, October 1978. 8/9.

"'The Romans' and The Establishment's Figleaf," *Guardian*, 3 November 1980. 12.

Guardian, 31 July 1981. 10.

Guardian, 16 January 1984. 9.

"Draft Introduction to 'The War Plays.'"

"Theatre Events," 4 & 11 January 1990.

"A Point of Dramatic Practice—TEs and Reality," 15 March 1990.

"Europe," 14 February 1990.

Comments to actors of "The Fool," *British Broadcasting Corporation,* 21 February 1990.

"Notebooks for 'Jackets,'" October 1989–March 1990.

Rehearsals of "Jackets II," October 1989–March 1990.

Final Notes to the London cast of "Jackets II," 26 February 1990.

Interviews/Discussions (given in chronological order).

Eltham Times, 29 November 1979. 53.

Auckland Star, 30 January 1980.

With Nick Philippou, undated.

With Nick Philippou, 16 November 1981.

With Calum MacCrimmon, undated.

With Stephanie Buschmann, 2 October 1987.

With author, 17 October 1989.

Lecture to the National Association for the Teaching of Drama Conference, October 1989. Transcript in *The Fight for Drama—The Fight for Education.* NATD Conference, ed. Ken Byron, April 1990.

Birmingham Post, 2 November 1989. 12.

With author, 14 December 1989.

The Times, 28 February 1990. 19.

With author, 12 June 1990.

With author, 22 December 1991.

Correspondence

Letter from Edward Bond to: the author, November 1983; 1 July 1985; 10 February 1990; 23 March 1990; 13 April 1990; 22 April 1990; 8 October 1990. Bas, Georges. 25 February 1989; 3 October 1989. Beck, Erika. 19 December 1986. Bond, Patricia. 15 March 1989. Chandler, John. 7 December 1989. Clemo, John. 12 February 1990; 9 March 1990. Eddershaw, Margaret. 3 February 1990; 4 April 1990; Klein Hagen, Hilde. 12 September 1987. Holloway, James. 1 December 1990. Jansen, David. 3 October 1989. Lamb, John. January 1982. MacCrimmon, Calum. 6 March 1989. Matheson, Philomena. 5 December 1989; 19 February 1990. Oakley, K. 21 April 1990. Paparassiliou, Vassilis. 25 August 1990. Pazardjiklian, Roberta. 5 January 1990. Philippou, Nick. 27 January 1990. *Plays and Players* (Editor.) 4 August 1991. Stafford-Clark, Max. 8 March 1990. Yefremov, Oleg. 13 February 1989.

Interviews (other than Bond)

Unpublished
Baron Cohen, Daniel. Personal Interview. 19 June 1990.

Bestwick, Debbie. Personal Interview. 26 June 1990.

Blanchard, Belinda. Personal Interview. 24 April 1990.

Blockey, Graham. Personal Interview. 14 May 1990.

Bryceland, Yvonne. Telephone Interview. 3 December 1989; 23 June 1990. Caulfield, John. Personal Interview. 15 January

1990. Church, Geoff, Personal Interview. 8 May 1990. Davis, Philip. Personal Interview. 29 January 1990. Dickson, Craig. Personal Interview. 25 April 1990. Eddershaw, Margaret. Personal Interview. 19 March 1990. Ford, Margaret. Personal Interview. 16 October 1989. Griffith, Eva. Personal Interview. 31 January 1990. Griffin, Hayden. Personal Interview. 21 February 1990. Hall, Peter. Personal Interview. 17 July 1990. Henson, Nicky. Personal Interview. 6 June 1990. Hildebrand, Dan. Personal Interview. 2 May 1990. Hooper, Robin. Personal Interview. 1 May 1990. Hudson, Tom. Personal Interview. Rehearsals, London 1990. Judd, Diana. Personal Interview. 13 April 1990. Kerr, Louise. Personal Interview. 20 April 1990. Laing, Stewart. Personal Interview. 3 May 1990. Legge, Janette. Personal Interview. 22 March 1990. McDiarmid, Ian. Personal Interview. 25 September 1989. Massey, Anna. Telephone Interview. 22 January 1990. Michell, Roger. Personal Interview. 4 April 1990. Morris, Maureen. Personal Interview. 7 March 1990. 4 October 1990. Philippou, Nick. Personal Interview, 15 December 1989; 9 March 1990. Price, Ken. Personal Interview. 20 April 1990. Roberts, Philip. Personal Interview. 13 December 1989. Russell Beale, Simon. Personal Interview. 5 February 1990. Ryall, David. Personal Interview. 2 November 1989. Shaw-Parker, David. Personal Interview. 11 September 1989. Stafford-Clark, Max. Personal Interview. 9 April 1990. Steed, Maggie. Personal Interview. 9 October 1989. Sturgess, Keith. Personal Interview. 19 March 1990.

Correspondence (other than Bond)

Unpublished
Tyrell, Norman. Letter to author, 5 February 1990.

Secondary sources

Amory, Mark. Rev. of *Summer*. *Spectator* 6 February 1982; 28.

Benjamin, W. *Illuminations*. London, 1970.

Bennett, Tony. *Formalism and Marxism*, London: Methuen, 1979.

Biddle, Margaret. "Learning and Teaching for Change and The Plays of Edward Bond." Diss. University of York, 1985.

Billington, Michael. Rev. of *The Worlds*. *Guardian* 17 June 1981: 10.

———, Rev. of *Restoration*. *Guardian* 22 July 1981: 12.

Bowden, Fran. Rev. of *Jackets II*. *Mansfield Chad*. 8 November 1989: 35.

Bryce, Jane. "Rehearsing Optimism," *Leveller* 10–24 July 1981: 18/19.

Bulman, James C. "'The Woman' and Greek Myth: Bond's Theatre of History." *Modern Drama* 29 (4) 1986: 505–15.

Callow, Simon. *Being an Actor*. New York: Grove Press, 1988.

Carlson, Marvin. *Theories of the Theatre*. Ithaca and London: Cornell University Press, 1984.

Cawood, Mal. "Whistling in the Wilderness," *Red Letters* (19) 1985: 11–23.

Cohn, Ruby. "The Fabulous Theater of Edward Bond." *Essays on Contemporary British Drama*. Munich: Hueber, 1981.

Coult, Tony. "Creating What is Normal." *Plays and Players*, December 1975: 9–13.

———, Background Material for 'Jackets': 1989.

Coveney, Michael. Rev. of *Summer*. *Financial Times* 28 January 1982: 21.

———, Rev. of *Restoration*. *Financial Times* 14 September 1988: 23.

de Jongh, Nicholas. Rev. of *Restoration*. *Guardian* 31 March 1989: 28.

Eagleton, Terry. *Marxism and Literary Criticism*. London: Methuen, 1976.

Esslin, Martin. "The Woman." *Plays and Players* 26 (1).

Frazier, Paul M. "Science Fiction Drama."' Diss. Michigan State University, 1988.

Figes, Eva. Rev. of *Summer*. *Times Literary Supplement* 5 February 1982: 133.

Gaskill, William. *Theatre at Work*, ed. Charles Marowitz and Simon Trussler. London: Methuen, 1967.

Hall, Peter. *Peter Hall's Diaries–The Story of a Dramatic Battle*, ed. John Goodwin. London: Hamish Hamilton, 1984.

Hay, Malcolm. "Edward Bond British Secret Playwright," *Plays and Players* June 1985: 8/9.

Hay, Malcolm and Philip Roberts. "Edward Bond: Stages in a Life." *Observer* Magazine, 6 August 1978: 12–13.

——, *Bond: A Study of his Plays*. London: Methuen, 1980.

Hirst, David L. *Edward Bond*. London: Macmillan, 1985.

Hostetter, Robert D. "Drama of the Nuclear Age," "Resources and Responsibilities in Theatre Education." *Performing Arts Journal* 11 1988: 85–95.

Hoyle, Martin. Rev. of *Restoration*. *Financial Times* 31 March 1989: 23.

Hudson, Christoper. Rev. of *The Worlds*. *New Standard* 18 June 1981: 26.

Hughes, G.E.H. "Edward Bond's 'Restoration.'" *Critical Quarterly* 25 (4) 1983: 77–81.

Hurren, Kenneth. Rev. of *Restoration*. *What's On In London* July 1981: 12.

——, Rev. of *Summer*. *What's On In London* February 1982: 23.

Innes, Christopher. "From Rationalism to Rhapsody." *Canadian Theatre Review* 23, Summer 1979: 109–113.

Jansen, David. "Working from 'Up Here.'" Diss. Royal Holloway and Bedford New College, May 1989.

Leiter, Samuel. *The Art of Kabuki*. Berkeley: University of California Press, 1979.

Lewis, Peter. *The National–A Dream Made Concrete*. London: Methuen, 1990.

Martin, M. "The Search for a Form; Recently Published Plays." *Critical Quarterly* 23 (4) 1981: 55–57.

Mathers, Pete. "Edward Bond Directs 'Summer' at the Cottesloe, 1982." *New Theatre Quarterly* Vol. 2, May 1986: 136–153.

Oliver, H. J., ed. *Timon of Athens*. By William Shakespeare. London: Methuen, 1979. xiii–lii.

Orgill, Douglas. Rev. of *Restoration*. *Daily Express* 22 July 1981: 3.

Poole, Mary. "The Dynamic of Contradiction in Selected Plays of Edward Bond: A Study in Dramatic Technique." Diss. Northwestern University, 1987.

Roberts, Philip. *Bond on File*. London: Methuen, 1985.

——, "The Search for Epic Drama: Edward Bond's Recent Work." *Modern Drama* 24 (4) 1981: 458–478.

——, "Edward Bond's 'Summer': a voice from the working class." *Modern Drama* 26 (2) 1983: 127–138.

Rubenstein, Richard. *Against the State*, BBC Radio 4, Wednesday May 2, 1990.

Rulewicz, Wanda. *A Semiotic Study of the Plays of Edward Bond*. Diss. University of Warsaw, 1987. Warsaw: Wydawnictwa Uniwersytetu Warszawskiego.

Scharine, Richard. *The Plays of Edward Bond*. Lewisburg: Bucknell University Press, 1976.

Shulman, Milton. Rev. of *Summer. Standard* 28 January 1982. 22.

Spencer, Charles. Rev. of *Restoration. New Standard* 23 July 1981: 25.

Spencer, Jenny Sue. "Edward Bond's Dramatic Strategies." *Contemporary English Drama,* 19 New York: Homes and Meier, 981: 123–137.

Stanislavsky, Konstantin. *An Actor Prepares* trans. Elizabeth Reynolds Hapgood. New York: Theatre Arts Books, 1952.

———, *Creating a Role* trans. Elizabeth Reynolds Hapgood. New York: Theatre Arts Books, 1949.

Willett, John. *Brecht on Theatre* trans., John Willett. London: Methuen, 1974.

Worth, Katharine. "Bond's 'Restoration.'" *Modern Drama* 24 (4) 1981: 479–493.

———, "Edward Bond." *Essays on Contemporary British Drama* Munich: Hueber, 1981: 205–222.

Young, B. A. Rev. of *The Woman. Financial Times* 11 August 1978: 17.

Index